DRIVE,
HE SAID

Jeremy Larner

A Delta Book • 1964

A Delta Book

PUBLISHED BY DELL PUBLISHING CO., INC.

750 THIRD AVENUE

NEW YORK, N.Y. 10017

COPYRIGHT © 1964 BY JEREMY LARNER

DELTA (R) TM 755118, DELL PUBLISHING CO., INC.

ALL RIGHTS RESERVED

LIBRARY OF CONGRESS CATALOG CARD NUMBER: 64-8038

TYPOGRAPHY BY IRENE ANNE YUSS

FIRST PRINTING

Grateful acknowledgment is made to the publishers and authors listed below for their permission to reprint material included in this volume: The poem, "I Know a Man" is reprinted with the permission of Charles Scribner's Sons from FOR LOVE by Robert Creeley. Copyright © 1962 by Robert Creeley.

"Bye, Bye Love" Copyright © 1957 by Acuff-Rose Publications, Inc. Reprinted by permission of Acuff-Rose Publications, Inc. "Sweet Georgia Brown" Copyright © 1925 by Jerome H. Remick & Company. Renewed and Assigned to Remick Music Corporation. Reprinted by permission of the Remick Music Corporation. "Talking Union" by THE ALMANAC SINGERS. Copyright © 1947 by People's Songs, Inc. Copyright © 1961 assigned to Stormking Music, Inc. Reprinted by permission of Stormking Music, Inc.

I hate, I despise your feast days,
And I will not smell in your solemn assemblies.

Woe to them that are at ease in Zion,
And are secure in the mountain of Samaria.

—AMOS *5:21, 6:1*

As I sd to my
friend, because I am
always talking,—John, I

sd, which was not his
name, the darkness sur-
rounds us, what

can we do against
it, or else, shall we &
why not, buy a goddamn big car,

drive, he sd, for
christ's sake, look
out where yr going.

I KNOW A MAN
—ROBERT CREELEY

She was going down the hill
At ninety miles an hour
When the chain
On her bi-
cycle broke.

They found her in the grass
With the sprocket up her ass
And her pretty
Tits punc-
tured by a spoke.

—American children's song

Chapter 1

➤ Every six hours the American satellite came from the underbelly of the globe and buzzed over the Island, movie-making. And now word came that the Enemy had a satellite up there, too, crossing the path of ours and spying on us! "Take down your spheroid of aggression or we will blast it from the Free World's atmosphere!" A peaceful people, Americans would nevertheless uphold their tradition of courage on the gridiron. Consequently we rushed observers to the Island to liberate its captive peoples. But the captive peoples turned out to be dupes, and were putting up resistance aided by Enemy instructors. The Enemy was known to have rockets at the ready, which would require "a full retaliatory response" if America were to observe her sacred trust. A U. S. naval blockade was swinging around the Island to cut off food shipments from our duplicitous allies. Helicopters dispatched from the secret training bases of Amalglopolated

9

Fruit and Progesteronic Oil had unofficially dropped coca-cola bombs defoliating the entire island.

But so far America was not involved. Nor was the Enemy. There had been no direct contact between satellites or between our observers and their instructors. Our leaders had taken a firm line. "We must not fight from fear, but neither must we fear from fight." To which the Enemy replied with a bluff: "To plug in our thermal heat bomb and burn the world to a cinder would be ashes in our mouth; nonetheless we cannot shrink from our commitments."

All over the world good citizens held their breath prayed to God and prepared themselves to stand up and go down for the vindication of right. Even at a small university upstate along the Hudson from New York City the crisis was felt. The thought of men dying had utterly unstrung young Hector Bloom. He had taken himself into a dream from which he couldn't wake, a dream of obligation and striving.

He dreamt he was an All-American basketball star, playing on Saturday afternoon nationwide TV interrupted now for an emergency bulletin. Warming up he could hardly see straight. Somewhere in the fieldhouse was the professor's wife with whom he was, in his dream, having an affair. She was sitting with her professor, and without looking passed him an empty bag of popcorn to dip his hand into. Her name was Olive Solomon, and the entire game was being played within her O.

It seemed there was a long history to the Hector Bloom of Hector's dream. He was not born 6-5 with brick-red fur on his head and the moves of a cornered cat. He had been a gamesplayer for years. Hours & hours as a little boy, long after the others had left the outdoor concrete court, Hector stayed on into the green & purple California twilight, dribbling, shooting, jumping, faking. Playing imaginary games with himself, O worthy opponent! He had formed out-wards around the grip he took on the American basketball. There was a moment between the rising and the coming-down—motion suspended and each cell motionless in a frenzy—when a steely calm fell sure upon Hector's fingers: the *grip*, the shot, the mesh of the net, the score. All prefigured in the ball and the grip, as the grown man all there in the microscopic sperm, gripping its curl so sweetly round the egg. The grip the shot the score the win. *Only O my Olive! When will I win a victory I can enjoy?*

Our national anthem. Fighting Coach Jack Bullion took him in his heartfelt arms. "We're counting on you, Big Hector. Don't let us down." *Lead our alliance. Put down the others.* His teammates crowded around Hector, some of them taller than he, pressing and patting. "Let's go to it, baby! You can do it, kid! Play 'em rough, Big Hector!" *We will fight them on the beaches.* Luther Nixon, student manager, towelled off Hector's elbows. "Go get 'em, Hector! Here's your chance to show those stupid sportswriters!" *We will fight them on the housetops.*

Off to the side stood the University's Negro, Thomas "Goose" Jefferson, the slickest guard in the East. He winked deadpan. "You'n' me, baby!" *We will fight them on the sportspage.*

Hector's hands were woven with the hands of his team-mates in a warm squirming pile of life. The commercial was over, and from on high came the signal to begin the game. "Okay, guys . . ." intoned Coach Bullion, smacking his beefy hands down on the pile. "We've got to have this one to stay alive. We lose, and we can kiss that tournament goodbye. We're not laying out those goddamn scholarships for nothing now! Let's play like we're supposed to for once. I hope you guys learned something from what you been hearing on the radio. Leave us not fear from fight!" *We will fight them on the networks.*

Coach Bullion glared straight across into Hector's lean tough face. Why weren't those eyes blue! For Hector's eyes were two red coals. "All right, Bloom!" (*YOU!*)

The crowd roared like sodium exploding as the five trotted to their ritual positions. The little ref came with his treasured globe tucked next his belly. Uuup went his little arms, like a baby boychild reaching for the moon. And he whistled, through his silver tongue: Play ball! Win game! *And we will nevah surrendah!*

Hector grabbed the ball and oh he threw a beautiful lovely pass downcourt. But his teammate wasn't looking. *Look at me, teammate! Did you think I would shoot? Not me.*

Up & down they ran, both teams fast-breaking. *Fitness for the legs!* Hector's friend the ball popped off the rim and he batted it back into the basket. Cheers. *He's really hustling out there, folks! I think.*

Time out for message. *Are we ahead or behind? Intelligence report: behind. Oh yes. Just have to play harder. Is that what Fighting Coach is saying? Words to that effect. Do they look at me strangely? Why? What?*

Goose Jefferson began shooting those long arching shots that curve so glamorous. Only they didn't go in. *Here I am, baby! Oh my baby!* Goose passed it right on the end of Hector's fingertips and Hector banked it in without even bothering to come down. *We must be even now. By rulebook we win since we're coming from behind. Unless we forget.*

Still asleep, Hector stole the ball. *Clever!* This was what he loved: dribbling down with one man between him and the basket. (*Poor bastard.*) Up in the air, fake once, fake twice, then slip ball under his arm for the basket. *Whoops! Fouled me, didn't you? Just apologize and I'll waive the freethrow.*

Pause. Hector Bloom on the foul line, ladies & gents, to complete his 3-point play. He always took his time to let the other team know he was in charge. Light with the fingertips and the ball zips through. Back on defense.

Hector was enjoying himself slightly now. Coach Bullion winced, gripped the bench till his hands went white. A weird dreamy grin had appeared on Hector's face.

Yes Hector was in his groove now, and Olive Solomon was watching. Down on the court, Hector's stubborn friend was driving. How determined he was, this friend, bouncing the ball and coming on, never giving up! His face all screwed up he faked and charged past Hector toward the basket. It was really too much trouble to get in his way. Hector let him by—then, as an afterthought, reached over his shoulder to block the shot.

Only after did Hector realize the risk. *Suppose he were really good? Once a good man gets inside you, he scores. Now Dr Morton Solomon is inside.* (Closeup of Solomon in the 16th row, tweed leg pressed against her knee.) *And oh he has scored! But I don't care. I can always score. To stop another man's score is a crime against beauty.*

Half-time. *This much again and it's all over.* (Except for next time.) Bodies slumped & lumped in the locker-room. Six-ten Butch Buckholder collapsed in despair over his tense play, tiny baby-face head limp atop plowhorse body. "Gee-miny Chris-mas!" Fingers Finnegan taking oxygen. Goose Jefferson standing, as usual, against wall. Never sat down till game was over. He avoided Hector's eyes. Each playing the pro, no time for sentiment. No joining together today. They were trying harder, somehow, and yet not trying hard enough. *Will we ever really hit it again together with joy, or are we truly now big-leaguers, grownup & grim?*

Perversely, Hector charged the barriers.

"Hey man, aren't you bothered by this crisis?"

Thomas Jefferson lifted an eyebrow.

"I mean with the satellites?"

Jefferson's eyes twinkled. He frowned. "Relax, man, you got to relax. You know what you look like out there? Relax, let it pass you by."

"Like the angel of death?"

"It will pass," Goose assured him. "Don't you mess with it."

Goose spanked Hector on the seat of his pants.

"Some folks never learn."

They must have fallen behind again. Fighting Coach had his blackboard out and madly drew diagrams. He would chalk plays on the floor if he could, *like Arthur Murray.*

"Are you listening, Bloom?"

"Are *you?*"

"But I'm talking!"

"Then you're not listening!"

Discord in the lockerroom. Angry growls. Threats. Directed toward redheaded athletic star lacking in proper motivation.

"Natural ability is one thing, Bloom," Coach Bullion informed him. "But there's something a real winner is never without. Us old-timers had a simple word for it: desire."

"And we will fight them on the beaches!" Hector shouted, Goose rushing to drag him off and quiet him.

Second half, same as the first/*little bit better & a little bit worse.* The cheerleaders bounced their skirts and chanted,

"Give 'em the ax, the ax, the ax!" And from the opposition: "Stomp 'em dead, green & red!" Plenty of grinding under the boards, where Hector would not have had to be if passes came sharper. Someone clutched at the bottom of his pants. And stepped on his foot. The game was deteriorating into football—shoving, blocking, grunting & kicking the ball out of bounds. The fast-breaking slowed into elaborate crisscrossing, as each team tried to shake a man free by setting up picks. Men collided in groups of three or four . . . one muscled clear . . . a shot. If it missed, a clatter of bodies under the boards. The players hung on each other's sweaty shoulders like galley slaves on a flagellation-break. Hector was tiring now, dreaming drearily, and twice lunged out for the ball, picking up his first two fouls and his first real cheers. *Hector Bloom, in there battling folks, for the glory of you!* (YOU!)

Like a machine Hector drove, shifted, dribbled through a hole, and at the last minute . . . got clobbered. Stood widespread on the foul line pulling in air . . . trying to wake himself up for the shot. Three men had fouled out in the process of tenderizing him, but due to his arrogance he sank sixteen out of seventeen freethrows. The seventeenth was unattainable, *like Olive up there or my own peace of mind.*

Coach Bullion was getting more & more panicky. At 7 points behind and two minutes to go, he told Hector to get out from the basket and start to pop. Hector shifted out as the guards drove in, took the blind shoulder pass from Goose, so dragged and done he let fly from instinct only and his grip on the ball. The long looped jump shot from way out like a glass of cold water after two hours of guerrilla infighting. Zip zip zip, three clean ones, *like mortar shells piercing the side of a tank,* letting in light,

15

bringing the weary crowd to a frenzy as a pressing defense nabbed the ball back each time. A jump ball was called with fifteen seconds to go and the home team 1 point behind. Hector knew they had it now and was dreaming past his dream, wandering delirious in the jungle of Olive Solomon's steaming green eyes. But there was still a piece of mechanics left.

Goose Jefferson snatched the tip and dribbled away five seconds practically horizontal, like a chocolate leaf blown across the floor. Then Hector came up from his corner, crossed behind him and took a shovel-pass.

Hector was laughing as he dribbled. Stopping, thrusting, faking, he faded like a ghost as he drove, straight for the basket. Three loomed up in front of him; he swerved, suspended in midair, at last a helpless target. For 1/10 of a second the crowd gulped terrified that he would not, could not get his shot away. Then a gasp as the ball came, not from over the outstretched sextet of hands, but from among their bodies, whipped behind Hector's back and through the maze to Goose Jefferson standing lonesome beneath the basket, loose as a goose. From his position on the floor with the three men heaped and tangled on top of him, Hector Bloom knew by the roar of delight that connections had been made and the performance ended satisfactorily.

As the trainer and three managers scraped him from the floor and began to drag him off to the sweathouse, Hector heard a familiar voice.

"Is he all right? Oh, I think he's hurt. He's hurt."

"He's all right, ma'am. Stand back please."

It was Olive, filing out with her husband and the rest of the fans. Hector couldn't even raise his head to see her.

They took him down into the heated atmosphere and threw him on the trainer's table, a collection of played-out bruises. *How sweet to lie and die on Caribbean beaches.* . . .

"Okay, man." Goose Jefferson's voice from far away. He felt the trainer kneading away at him, restoring the property. Slowly he was coming awake now. . . .

Fighting Coach Jack Bullion entered. "At last, son, you're showing us what you got inside of you! That's the stuff we want to see! You're gunna make it now, son, you're a real pro!"

Hector Bloom was awake. He had never been asleep. This game was not a dream, it was his life.

Chapter 2

Had you stepped into the showers after the winning of the game, you would have observed with no small curiosity a ceremonial in progress.

Not the wondrous physiques, nor the prodigious limbs, nor the miracle of sleek youth, would so interest you as half a glimpse of that unaccountable dangle which proceeds downward in all but the most favorable weather.

Thus—beyond the towel-flipping, the soap-flinging, the screams and jostles that accompany a victory—a meticulous examination was taking place. With its chief object the above-mentioned instrument.

A costly relique, indeed, and one that could likely have become detached in the conflict just ended. It was necessary to assure oneself, for which purpose a baptism, with laying on of hands.

Fingers Finnegan turned his inside out, reaming it with a bar of soap. Butch Buckholder scrubbed mightily, both hands plunged up to the elbow, an expression of absent-mindedness taxing his brow. Rodney Jellop fastidiously laved and separated each tufty fiber. It was important that if the apparatus had in any respect retreated or diminished itself under the pressure of action, it now be restored to its full dimensions, stretched rubbed washed fluffed freed and flourished.

The existence of an international crisis did not in any respect modify this occasion. To the contrary.

Basic equipment inspected and found in order, the celebrants moved to comparison. Jellop had a clear claim to length, but perhaps Jeff Crasby had the edge in thickness. Thomas Jefferson's was of another color. Jellop sported a scallop, Finnegan's came and went again, Buckholder's veered sharply, Tony Lupini's tapered.

Individual differences are the bread and wine on the table of democracy. Though one might outclass another, as a team they hung together, hoisting a collective banner of triumph. Symbolically, each made claim on the other, with wet towels flicked in play, innocent gestures, comradely jokes.

What's a joke? If it's a joke, nothing will happen. That's the rules of the game.

"Mary, get *out* of my shower!"

"But Mary, I thought you were one of us!"

In turn, this too is washed away with soapy laughter. Joke: Coach Bullion wraps his in cellophane. Noise, cold water, raising of the voice in song.

Ritual completed, a general rush for the lockers, relaxed, washed up, looking to clothe themselves with care, to ease tired bodies into the twilight, rest weary hulks on jumpy blondes.

Dragging to the shower as they fled, one Hector Bloom,

delayed by trainer. "Hec-tor Bay-bee!" In passing, a pounding of the back.

Beginning, bleary-eyed, his private ablutions, Hector Bloom observed once more his own claim to distinction. Symmetric, triple-jointed, well in trim with ancient tribal specifications. A prominent member of society. Still, for all that, something was missing, and once more he searched for it.

Chapter 3

————————————————➤ Hector retired to his room, thinking to sleep through supper.

Unlike the other athletes, who lived in pillared fraternity houses, Hector Bloom made his home in a tiny caretaker's room in the bowels of the gymnasium. To the distress of Fighting Coach and the whole Athletic Dept he forswore fresh air and sociability to live with his friend Gabriel Reuben, who worked out his Politics Dept scholarship by stoking the furnace and pushing the long dustmop across the gym floor at half-time. Gabriel was a New York boy with legs slender as toothpicks, long as Hector's but so stiltlike it seemed he might be blown off his feet by the draught of an opening door. His upper body was truncated by caved-in shoulders, but his head, held delicately on a graceful neck, was beautiful and even inspiring. His eyes in particular were fine ones, gentle & bright, and his broad forehead was crowned by a thatch of curling blond hair.

Gabriel was the only child of a careful-shrewd father

who stayed comfortably middle-class even after investing himself past his first million dollars and a careful-clean mother who had nearly had a breakdown getting him born. (There was so much mess!) Strangely enough—despite his parents never giving him anything he didn't need and warning him how spoiled he was—little Gabriel became something of a problem child. Yes, he was a nasty kid all right, and for the well-being of the household he was sent to Arizona boarding schools in the wintertime and on supervised fishing treks etc to Canada in the summer. When Gabriel went trekking the counselors had to broil him steaks every night . . . or else Gabriel wouldn't eat. They tested him once and he went three days and started to die on them. Naturally his fellow trekkers hated him, but it was hard not to love him when he caught a fish: he was so deliriously happy.

In the form of a child, Gabriel could never quite pull himself together. But soon enough his life began to take a definite (& startling) shape: the revelation of Gabriel as the son of God. At twelve years of age Gabriel, to the despair of his would-be parents, declared himself an Anglo-Catholic. For the next three years he worshipped a life-size luminous crucifix on his bedroom wall and took private communion from an engraved silver chalice he had secured for $300 at an antiquary on 57th Street. (His life's savings —Gabriel played for keeps, even then.) Every Sunday Gabriel went unattended to the Anglican High Ceremony, where his great Hebrew eyes shone archangelic among the pallid Anglos & Saxons of the choir.

When Gabriel went to college he became Chairman of the Board. He possessed & displayed twenty-three cashmere sweaters, charcoal bermuda shorts with a belt in the back plus blazer, an initialed platinum hipflask, a car that played music of sophisticated violins and made up into a bed, and doll-girls to fit casually inside the car. Before long Gabriel was elected President of the Inter-Fraternity Social Committee, and suavely officiated at the Coronation of the Winter Passion Queen. For an instant he almost had his parents impressed (O vain dream of every dream-seized middle-class son!), and Gabriel grabbed that instant to insist that his father release certain monies deposited in Gabriel's name so Gabriel could use them to speculate in satellite missile stocks.

In the Spring of Gabriel's Sophomore year, alas, the Enemy launched a brief- & devastating "peace offensive," which reduced Gabriel to farthings. Tired of himself, Gabriel took the disaster as a sign that the Gods, too, were bored with his corporate mode. And thus it came to pass that at the onset of the summer which would have marked the halfway point in his never-to-be-finished college career, Gabriel found himself with three months at home stretching ahead of him like an old age and the need to change his style becoming more anguished every day. His old friends revulsed him, but left alone he grew deeply depressed. For when the sons of God are not high, high as angels, they wallow in mucky despair and are as nothing to themselves. Gabriel felt himself incapable of emotion— neither thing nor person could arouse a sensation in him. When people tried to talk to him, he stared back in horror and retired to the bathroom where he would spend hours in reverie staring at the face imprisoned behind glass, puzzling who it was and what meant for. Once out of the bathroom, his anxiety took him anew: he was afraid that the face in the glass had been ripped out from behind and torn into shreds.

As usual it was a question of who would crack up first, Gabriel or his mother. He won: eight days after his homecoming she put on an incomparable display of hysterics. Rather pleased, Gabriel in the wake of her seconal readily promised to see a psychiatrist.

After a few days of searching, Gabriel walked into the office of a biotherapist.

"Sit down!" commanded Dr Fulton Macher, watching him intently. "No, in that chair over there!"

Suddenly Dr Macher jumped to his feet. "Why did you start?" he inquired. "Don't tell me, let me tell you. You don't know what role to take, do you? I can tell by mere observation of your body. You think you can't be seen through, but to the trained eye you give yourself away with every move of your musculature. You're beginning to resent me now, aren't you? You think perhaps I will reach across the desk and *strike you!*"

With the words *"strike you!"* Dr Macher slammed an Oriental statuette against the wall, sending Gabriel leaping to the top of a hat tree. There followed a series of amazing revelations.

For Mrs Reuben's $35/hr, the biotherapist began to ease Gabriel in the direction of Affirmative Posture and True Orgasm. In True Orgasm—the key to free-flowing love & creativity—the body moves as freely as a freely swinging leg. While Gabriel stood naked in the middle of the room, describing how beautifully bothered he was, the therapist moved around him, thumping and prodding. Occasionally Dr Macher massaged Gabriel's leg muscles to loosen them up, and once he took off his shoes and worked on Gabriel's back with his bare feet.

Gabriel was willing and had much to say, but when results were slow appearing he was discouraged and talked of quitting and simply taking *karate* lessons. Perhaps it was his talent for meeting the right people at the destined time that pulled him through for the moment; at any rate it was the people he met who helped him turn more & more swinging, and his legs swung right along with him. The biotherapist's studio was located in a choice part of the Village, and hanging around certain bars Gabriel managed to contact newer & holier people than he had ever known existed. The first were the great actor Tony Valentine and his mad poet brother Billy-Gene Valentine. Tony was also an Orgasm man, but more than that he gave Gabriel his first fuzzy intimations of how the orgasm might be just one feature of a hitherto-unthoughtof psychic politics that could swing our desperate world into a new wild millennium of pleasure. Historically, said Tony, this had to be; the organism renews itself or perishes. For the individual, the title to such vision could come only through experience—and so Gabriel made himself available for a number of scenes with spade chicks, drag queens and certain selected studs. He did not kid himself that he was making it all the way.

It was enough to know that he was with it. Through Tony & Billy-Gene, Gabriel met painters, poets, hustlers, boosters, roosters, horse riders and magicians—all of whom seemed mostly *to exist*, and to exist so vividly that those who lived for any other reason became mute, impalpable and invisible to the young Gabriel. Jazz itself came to him, the Negro night come alive and burning pain joy *real*, not to be tricked, cutting in an edge of sheer hot beauty through the torpid blanket of daytime lies. When Gabriel shut his eyes and climbed inside, he *knew*—and, like the blues, he was a cure for himself. And when the music stopped, well, he still had something left, enough to go on with. . . . *Dayenu.*

When fall came Gabriel forswore his parents' support and went back to college car-less and nearly clothes-less. Immediately upon getting off the bus he resigned from his fraternity and got down to work. He knew he had a lot to learn. He wanted to travel the path of every revolutionary in history, to plot the spiral on which they swung, and to ride that curve out into the future. He studied hard, and before long he had earned himself his work-scholarship and his caretaker's room in the gym. The only problem was people. His former collegiate friends were as interesting to him as stiffs in a morgue. Equally dead were the officially good students, some of whom he knew were much more proficient than himself, because they tried so trustingly to be "rational"—i.e., to force whole sets of old learned vocabularies between themselves and the lives they were leading. Like little children stamping their feet at life because it is not all them, or all theirs. Open your eyes! screamed Gabriel, in every way he knew. Gabriel wasn't rational and he knew it. He was after something realer and larger than the definitions of words.

Gabriel needed a hero of destiny, if only to know more clearly his own destiny. With unerring instinct he fastened upon Hector Bloom.

Gabriel worshipped Hector because in Hector dwelt the energy he knew as the blood-spirit. In propitiation to that force in Hector larger than them both, Gabriel painted on the cinder-block wall of their room a bloody sign:

SQUARE—SELF CONTROL
HIP—THE RIGHT REACTION

He knew his man.

There was huge strength in Hector. Gabriel was staggered with love at the sight of Hector's daily onslaught on the world, both on and off the basketball court. The onslaught was massive, for Hector Bloom had good reason to hate, and good reason or no his enormous heart was clogged with hatred, both auricle & ventricle.

Why Hector loved Gabriel was harder to say. He was so tired of people who talked. . . . And Gabriel talked more than any of them. . . .

When Hector passed among the boilers and climbed the steps to their room, he found Gabriel standing before a mirror, painting a bird on his bare chest in watercolors. An amazing eagle, wings laid back and soaring.

"Gorgeous!" Hector exclaimed.

Gabriel threw his paint kit under his bed, laughing. "Some bit, isn't it? I get hung up waiting for you. Like I don't want to split without you, but I don't feel like reading and masturbation leads to insanity, man, you know that."

Hector stretched out on his bed. "No you don't, baby!" shouted Gabriel, tugging at Hector's arm to no effect. "It's time to go!"

"Go where?"

"I don't know, man," Gabriel said, going into a glum shuffle with his hands jammed rigid in his pantspockets, staring at his big helpless shoes. "I can't think about anything but these little bureaucrats and their buttons. I mean what's the point of lying down, man? This could be the end and here you are cooling it!"

Hector got up. "An orgy," he said: "That's how we ought to go! If only I had time to print some invitations!"

"Look," said Gabriel. "Tony's speaking here tonight, on campus. Afterwards there's going to be some cats at Conrad Hurvey's. We're going to talk it over. I mean this is it, we're not just playing around anymore. If the tin soldiers don't blow up the whole works, we're going to have a fucking *revolution!*"

"What kind of revolution is a fucking revolution?"

Gabriel laughed, and pounded Hector a shot in the arm. "Don't know, man, maybe it's like where everyone can freely fuck everyone else."

"I thought we had that already," Hector said.

"Oh we have sex all right, man, all over the place. In your clothes, your magazines, your big pricky cars with their chrome cunts. That's what they dish out to keep us in line, like recess for the kiddies, dig—line up and keep quiet or we won't let you out. But they blow that whistle, man, the kids come trotting and *you* know, nobody fucks anymore, I mean really *fucks*. Fuck *up*, yes, like you did in the game tonight, but not honest-to-god fuck."

They were out of the gym and walking across the parking lot.

"Maybe we should go talk to Morton Solomon," said Hector slyly, ". . . since he's your advisor and everything. He ought to be able to explain the politics of what's happening."

"You mean give us a lot of shit about 'strategy'!" And then write what we said in his secret files! Don't put me on at a time like this, man! Of course you wouldn't mind a little conference with his wife."

"Wouldn't I?"

"Not that I can blame you, man. I dig her. I like chicks who can *move*. Hey, do you remember when we were freshmen and she was still dancing here? Crazy! She was supposed to be lewdness and she was *lewd!* Only I don't dig her scene with Dr Morton. You know I doubt they even fuck. You know dancers don't care for it too much, except with other dancing-chicks. Maybe that's why she got herself that leftover from the thirties, that Ivy-League Lenin!"

". . . who taught you everything you know!"

". . . but nothing to do, man, nothing to do! He didn't teach me, he just gave me words!"

Many cars still remained in the fieldhouse parking lot, their occupants having strolled a quarter-mile to the Theatre Arts Compound, where an audience was already collecting to hear the notorious Tony Valentine. But Hector climbed aboard his fire-engine red convertible that he got for signing while he was still in high school, four years old by now & beaten. He wanted to cruise out the twilight before submitting himself to a lecture. He started the car and waited; Gabriel was fussing around somewhere at the back of the lot. Finally he appeared and climbed in, chuckling, rubbing his hands together.

"See that big mother back there?" he said. "That's Solomon's new car."

"What gives with you & him?" asked Hector. "I thought he was your favorite."

"Don't bug me, baby. Bad enough that cat should get

himself named Dean of Men. But do you know what he told me today? He's going to the Capitol. Joining up with the Powers!"

"No!" Hector was shocked.

"Yes. Independent thinker shoots straight for the gravy. I told him, 'Honored teacher, by that one act and that act alone, you've given me a definition of liberalism.' So he explains to me that These Are Exciting Times To Be Alive, that the high poobahs respect his Ideas, that it's his Responsibility To Do What He Can. I told him, 'Honored teacher, you're going to climb the cock of power! From now on, you zero with the rest of the zeros!'"

"And what did he say?"

"He looked over his shoulder and said, 'Don't be naive, Mr Reuben.'"

Hector wondered how this could be true. He knew that Morton Solomon knew his politics, not only from the journals he now wrote for, but from the streets of New York, where at college age he was already editing a labor paper and addressing mass rallies. Solomon was a city kid from the start, depression-tough and dialectic-wise—a figure of wonderment and awe to Hector Bloom, half-hick, half-Jew, lefthanded neurotic basketball player from the green hills of California.

Morton Solomon had spent World War II as a company clerk in Sicily, and come back tougher than ever. He'd entered academic life as an ex-radical, calling himself a liberal but scorning other liberals. He had written a much-discussed book on the uses of "deliberate limited military intervention" as an "effective modern" postwar policy—a book that had reputedly "caught the imagination" of our country's leaders. The book took a mocking tone towards policies of dabble and compromise. Solomon was not against

30

compromise, he explained to his students; he knew what life was—but he expected that men of political intelligence ought to have a damn clear idea of what they were compromising for.

Well, thought Hector, *I guess* HE *knew. Now what else does he know?*

But Hector felt relieved, strangely justified. He, too, was remembering Olive dance, but not as lewdness. She was in the middle of the floor, dancing an incredible Russian dance in which the dancer spins and stamps and kicks and jumps and spins while the music bangs harder and faster. The other dancers—who a moment before had been stepping through a mambo—stood rooted in a circle and clapped and stared at the flashing of her lovely slender legs. She had come as a chaperone, quiet, nervous they thought, sensitive-looking, laughing nodding nervous, clinging to the arm of her husband for the first two hours. Then some friends of hers had jumped on the bandstand with Russian instruments and she had started to dance, slowly at first, and then faster as the spirit possessed her and took her beyond herself. Hector was thrilled, felt his blood run warm: as she turned once, twice, to the same place, eyes shining bright and then obscured by the whipstream of hair: *how she enjoyed herself!* She left the earth with her grace. She had won her victory, and Hector yearned to go along with her.

She had seen him watching. Later she came right up to him, with such enormous completeness!

"Walk with me," she had said.

"Who, me?"

In his car. That was the first time and she was way ahead of him, dancing yet, rejoicing in her power. She held his head with tenderness, compassion almost, and he felt stuck in the mud and hopeless. He would never catch up to her, never share with her what she alone had. What she had alone.

"But I am," she laughed. "I am perfectly happy."

She shook her black fall of hair behind her and brought her lips to his.

She had to run. Turning the rearview mirror, she expertly put on lipstick. She tied up her hair, pulled on her heels, kissed him on the back of his hand, and ran teetering from the car back toward the light and into the life she had leapt so abruptly out of.

"Paradise Squat!" Gabriel swore. "Don't put me on, Hector, she must be cold as an iceman's shoulder. It's no accident who you marry, dig? Now I ponder it I doubt altogether they fuck."

"No one fucks anymore," Hector said.

"That's right, man. Only just remember I was the first to see it!"

They were heading back toward campus now. Gabriel glanced repeatedly at his wristwatch as Hector pulled again into the parking lot.

"No, man!" said Gabriel abruptly. "Over that way!" He nearly grabbed the wheel. "Over that way!"

"But why?"

"You'll see in a minute." Gabriel checked his watch again.

As they headed up the path towards the Theatre Arts Compound, an orange explosion pierced the new night, raising a small cloud of debris back in the parking lot.

"What was that?" asked Hector.

"Car explosion. No one in it."

"Car explosion!"

"Wouldn't be surprised," said Gabriel.

Chapter 4

—————————➤ Luther Nixon strutted to
the podium wearing a red vest and brass buttons beneath
his tidy suit. In addition to his job as Head Manager, this
leader of tomorrow was President of the Student Body.

"When we think of a guy like Tony Valentine," said
young Nixon, "we see an American youth standing on
the deck of a schooner in the South Seas. A man with a
dream."

"Christ!" said Tony Valentine, sitting behind him.

Luther Nixon joined modestly in the laughter.

"We think of a sailor who became an actor, yes, but we
also think of an actor who flew a Navy dive bomber for
his country in World War II. We think of an amateur
boxer, a thinker in his own way, and of a boy from Brooklyn
who had the Enterprise to become a Hollywood Star. Ladies
and gentlemen, when I was told I was to have the honor
of . . ."

"All right, all right!" Tony Valentine shuffled forward, grinning at Luther Nixon with his sea-beaten blue eyes. "I'm going to throw up!"

There was a hubbub of applause, led longest by Tony's claque up front, which included his brother Billy-Gene and a bald, stocky man whom Hector supposed to be Conrad Hurvey. Hector was standing in the back with Goose Jefferson and Hector's professor of classics, young Dr Richard Calvin. Gabriel had joined his girl Claudine.

"You know, I sympathize with you young moviegoers. You went out and got yourself an entertainer and here you are, waiting to be entertained. Well, I ain't gonna do it.

"You! Stick that notebook up your ass! I'm not *material!* You see before you your *demon*, and either I'm going to get to you or you're going to get to me!"

"Yeah!" said Hector.

So instead of ogling a movie star, the audience got itself insulted and sworn at. Tony invited them to fight back, but they weren't used to it. Every time someone asked a question, Tony buttered it with his beautiful incoherent romantic anarchism, and rubbed the asker's nose in it. He told them that to be an American college student was to be a good little doggie getting paper-trained. Learning rules. To live, to be truly alive, was to make your own rules. And to walk straight over anyone who told you he was your Ruler.

"Doesn't this imply violence?" asked Richard Calvin, teasingly.

"Aw come on, Richard! This cat is standing here with a million tons of TNT floating over his head and he's scared he might have to punch someone in the nose! You mean we ain't got violence right now? Why man, we're about to fold up the whole show! Which is better, that manicured

34

finger on the trigger, or each man slugging it out face-to-face for the way he wants to be?"

"Don't give me deterrence!" he bellowed at a member of the debating team. "Deterrence is a word. That's the trouble with you, you're sick with words. Look. We give you a college education to save us, we're crying out to be saved, to be led from the wilderness. But could you lead us? No, you're born followers, pumped full of words. If only you were capable of *feeling* one beautiful thing! . . .

"You've been bribed! You've sold your hookey privileges for a play period!

"What we need in every city street is a screaming saint to remind us *not* to follow leaders. *Any* leaders! We need *dis*loyalty. Subversion. Anarchy. Every man for himself."

"But society will collapse!"

"I know, I know, baby; society will collapse." Tony grinned, ground his fist into his palm. "But maybe *you* won't collapse, baby, maybe for the first time in your life you'll *make it!*

"*How* do you make it? Who asked how? Who? I don't know how you'll make it, young lady, you've got to make it your own way, like Hector Bloom plays ball!

"Tell me, you pretty people, why are you alive? What are you doing here?"

"Getting some discipline!" a budding man of letters answered.

"But you don't *get* discipline, man, discipline you give yourself—when you got something worth disciplining. Do you think I learned to act by getting myself disciplined? What you need is *freedom*, so you can *be* something! Yes, I know, freedom is scary. You might plunge to the bottom of the pit. And there you'd find death, because death's at

35

the bottom of everything. You might not come out alive. But if you did, you'd have a life worth living! That's what death is for! Don't you think you can live? Or do you prefer the living death of sleepwalkers? Why not take a chance? Don't you believe in people?"

Dr Richard Calvin was laughing, taunting. "Are you trying to convert us?" he called. "What's the difference between you and a square? Why don't you leave us free? Don't you believe in people?"

Tony sputtered and his words were drowned in a fury of accusation from the audience.

Richard Calvin turned to Hector. "The man's rhetoric is first-rate," he said behind his hand. "What can you do with such a fellow—let him grow up? *That's* the charge he should make against America—it didn't let him grow up!"

Tears burnt in Hector's eyes. "I think I'm going to lay you out," he told his classics professor.

"Easy now," said Goose from his other side. (Goose, too, was laughing.) But a fresh disturbance distracted them.

Dean Morton Solomon was demanding the floor. "I have something of grave importance to announce." He came up and stood on the stage with Tony Valentine.

"Word came five minutes ago from the Capitol. The Enemy has agreed to withdraw its satellite, if we orbit ours within the prescribed boundaries. There may be further skirmishes on the Island, but for the moment The Crisis is over!"

"And so am I," said Tony. But no one heard him in the cheers of relief that were resounding. The more patriotic students burst into song. They sang the school fight song, for the line had been held.

Hector joined the little group up front near the stage.

Tony had come down and was shaking hands. Looking shyly now from his boy's blue eyes, he asked Morton, "Now that it's over, do you believe any of it was real?" Morton smiled knowingly, ironically. "Frankly, no." Tony shrugged and turned away. He brushed Olive and amazingly they reached out and pinched each other's behinds. *Not sexually but how?* Hector was astonished, but in the action that followed he forgot what he had seen. Tony moved on without a backward glance, followed by his entourage and besieged by autograph collectors.

Gabriel had captured Hector and was hauling him away. "This doesn't change a thing!" he whispered. "We're still meeting."

Getting Hector away from the crowd, he hugged his arm elatedly. "You know Tony was at the game tonight!" Gabriel told him. "He digs you!" *He would.*

Meanwhile Billy-Gene Valentine came slinking onstage from the wings, bare-shouldered, wearing an American flag as a sarong.

The audience froze in its departure, stared aghast at this bony, hairy-legged Tiresias.

Billy-Gene cupped his arms behind his head, tilted back his chin, and swaying his hips recited a brief poem:

God is dead.
Drive, He Said.

He went into a luxuriant bump and grind, spreading himself invitingly, hoping in vain that the audience would come down and devour him.

Chapter 5

━━━━━━━━━━━━━━▶ Conrad Hurvey had rent-
ed the basement of a bowling alley in the Bronx. Hector
and Gabriel passed through the stares of late-night bowling
hoods and went down a flight of concrete steps. They halted
by a golden door.

After a long pause a voice from behind the door croaked,
"Who? Who?"

They entered into a dark cellar which stretched clam-
mily away from them. Lit by the flicker of a tall pink
candle, a mattress lay on the concrete floor, its ticking
scarred by a crimson stain. As their pupils widened, they
made out the outline of a screen at the far end of the basement. Their guide took them across the concrete through
an atmosphere which grew thicker with every step. Behind
the screen was a King Arthur round table, where a number
of faces grouped around a dim oil lamp in the ritual passing
of roaches.

Hector introduced himself by reaching up and pulling the chain which snapped on an overhead lightbulb. The roach-passers shrunk away from the light. "Oh man, man! Off with it, man!" But Tony said, "That's OK," rubbing his eyes, and Gabriel said, "No, we need some light for our planning."

There were not many people for the occasion. Hector noticed a masked man, a Negro with shades, goatee, formal mustache and beret pulled low so that his face was inaccessible. Attached to him was a tiny chick in leotards. Billy-Gene Valentine lay with his tousled head on the table, and did not stir the whole time. Conrad Hurvey was short, swart, wore black close pants with no cuffs and a tweed cap, and at every word Tony Valentine uttered gave out with a sly cool chuckle, as if to say, you'n'me, Tony kid, we got it made. Under Gabriel's elbow sat their guide, a small man stoned out of his mind, Irving Dormowz, whose small brown felt-covered head just made it over the top of the table, and who stared mightily from either huge goggled eyes or small goggled glasses. Calmly sifting out the tea was Gabriel's girl Claudine, who lowered her eyes modestly, as quiet as a cat. She did not crave attention; Hector had known her to sit still and alert while the men went off on a three-hour laugh flight comparing orgasms or recalling old baseball stars and radio programs.

In fact, they had just finished the re-creation of a dozen late afternoon adventure serials. The masked man, whether from this night or before, was known as Captain Midnight. He sat toying with his blade as Conrad Hurvey got launched on a play-by-play of a Western he had seen that week. While he talked, Claudine quietly rolled and passed fresh tea-sticks. Hector drew deep on his and sucked the smoke down under his diaphragm. He liked marijuana when he could get it; he had no visions, but it soothed him, and soothing was for Hector a far more valuable reward.

"So check this, Tony. The cat is sitting there with his rod, dig? And the gorilla moves in on him, step by step. The camera is down below, dig, so like when he's over him he's blotting out the sky. *Huge* gorilla! Then WHAM! Like that: you see this fantastic hole blasted right through his stomach!"

Conrad gave his wheezy laugh.

"Just WHAM! And man, like you can see daylight through that cat's insides! Dig it, Tony?"

Tony laughed and said Crazy! and then the others laughed.

"Like this you mean!" shouted Gabriel, whipping out a pistol. "WHAM WHAM WHAM!" he screamed, and three spitballs came popping out at suddenly-white Conrad Hurvey.

Captain Midnight turned his head to see, and all in a flurry they gathered round Gabriel. All but Billy-Gene, who still slept, for it was not his hour. Gabriel brought his piece forward to Tony, little Irving fondling it from underneath.

"It's a gas, hey?" said Gabriel.

"A real gasser," Tony said.

Tony had come near Hector and was looking at him from the corners of his old sailor's eyes. It was the quick once-over Hector always got from the man who was set to guard him in the big game and who wouldn't let on for an instant that he had spent all week watching films and charting Hector's every move.

"Can't figure whether you're genius or magician . . . ," mumbled Tony, half turning away.

"Are you talking to me?" inquired Hector.

Tony flushed, might have said something, but not quite.

"I'm a bum," Hector said, but the moment had passed. Everyone shifted as a new man entered, a man dressed in a plain leather jacket, like a workingman, a stocky, solid individual whose square straightforward face was deeply furrowed and whose grey hair stuck up in a bush.

"This is Robert Frank, from the Pacifist Committee," announced Gabriel, suddenly formal.

"Fact, he's an old old war-buddy of mine," Tony said, and Robert Frank smiled and laid one tough hand on Tony's shoulder. He looked to be twenty-five years older than Tony, who was in his forties.

"I have disturbing news," said Robert Frank. "On the assumption that Enemy agents are hiding among the crops, our observers on the Island are firing the countryside. Of course all kinds of people are hiding in the fields, and they are dying in great numbers. Some of them are hiding there because they don't want to live behind barbed wire in our Freedom Villages. There is no place else to hide because we have burned their huts to forestall guerrilla action. When our Committee marched in peaceful protest in Times Square, the policemen panicked and rode their horses into our picket lines. Many of us were badly beaten then and later at The Tombs. I saw one woman stabbed in the groin with a billy as they threw her into the paddy wagon, and another had her skull fractured when a horse stepped on her head."

"That's cool," said Captain Midnight.

"It's like we were saying," Gabriel burst out. "If there's ever going to be a time, this is it. New scenes are popping all over the world. Everywhere you look, it's either a revolution or a fascist army take-over. It has to be one or the other, dig, no in-between, the pressure is just too much. How can you let a peasant have a *little* land: that's ludicrous, give him a taste and he'll want everything he's got coming. It's that collective unconscious, coming closer to the top every day! Every moment more and more people are choosing sides: some go right, to the fucking fascists, and some go left, for a people's revolution. And that's where we come in: all we do is step on the scene.

"Because goddammit man there's going to be a fucking REVOLUTION in this country! I believe in it man, this rubber-dumpling shit can go on only so long. When you bring that collective unconscious to a boil, BANG it explodes! Today, tomorrow, anyday!"

"Check," Tony said. "But don't you think we should talk it over and decide on some objectives?"

"No, man! What is there to talk about? I mean nothing has happened yet. The minds of the poor people are still tranquillized. When they come to and see what's been put on them, there's got to be blood, man, blood in the streets. Got to be! The question is *whose?* If we don't watch out, why not ours? The only thing we can do now is every man do what he can to get it started, then from there on we act together. We just have to be ready. But none of this bureaucratic shit, man. A revolution shapes itself in action, and when it begins to do that, *then* we can talk. Right now we take our chances. Like look: you're hung up on your self-defense classes so you *have* your self-defense classes; I'm hung up with this star business so let that be *my* hangup. Dig? Stay in touch, stay cool, and *cook!*"

Gabriel was agitated. With every word his long neck whipped his head back and forth and his forefinger rent the air like a knife. Hector looked at Robert Frank and saw the man's incredible furrows deepen.

"Right!" said Conrad. "When can we make it for your classes, Tony?"

"How about Monday night?"

"No, I can't," Gabriel said.

"Then some other night."

"No, never mind about me, I can take care of myself. Just go ahead, that's the main thing."

"But I can't come then either," croaked Irving.

"Then Tuesday night."

"No good for me," said Conrad.

By chance there was no night when all of them could get together for Tony's classes in self-defense.

"What are the stars?" Hector asked Gabriel.

"Simple, man. They're fucking little white stars. Like each one has in the middle of it a flag with the words, The American Revolution. I get them printed at this place I know and we stick them all over—busses, sidewalks, fucking mailboxes. . . ."

"And what does that accomplish?" asked Robert Frank.

"Man it's something the people can *see*, and know they're not fucking alone, and like act."

". . . like act," repeated Frank.

Tony picked up *The New York Times Sunday Magazine*, which had been lying on the table, and thumbed through the ads. He held up a big color photo of a slim brown man and a matching slim brown woman, both in bathing suits and eating from a pyramid of California prunes.

"Let's see now," said Tony with his famous wry smile. "Let's have a little practice placing the star." He handed the magazine to Claudine. "Now where would you put the star on this one?"

Claudine froze. "Where?"

"Like where on the model?"

The leotard-girl pounced. "I'd put it here!" she cried, jamming her finger on the man's groin.

"Yes . . . yes," murmured Claudine.

"I wouldn't," said Conrad slyly. "I wouldn't put it on the model at all. I'd put it on the brand name."

"Let's be specific. Just where on the brand name?"

Gabriel was pacing violently around the room, stopping twice in each circuit to bend back double sucking pot-smoke into his lungs, then resuming his journey, in and out of the dark border the shadow of the screen made. Trancelike voices quavered. Gabriel put a record on and wild jazz flared up from the dark. Gabriel came dancing out into the bulb-light, twisting and wheeling scrunching and unscrunching his body with cheeks puffed and fingers crawling on the keys of his imaginary saxophone.

"Who am I?" he demanded of Hector.

"Ornette?"

Shook no. Busily blowing.

"Gerry Mulligan?"

"You kidding?"

"No, I give up."

A look of hurt disappointment. "Coltrane!" Continued blowing & wheeling.

"Look Tony," Conrad said, "if we're gonna train people to use the hands etcetera I think we ought to train them in the use of small arms, too."

Tony looked calm & potful. "All right, good idea."

"I know a place where we can get as many as we like."

"Crazy."

"In the meantime," broke in Gabriel from his horning, "I'm gonna get those fucking stars printed up tomorrow!"

It had been a long day. All the tiredness of the game came over Hector, only peacefully, through the haze of Mary-

Jane, and he felt like laying himself down in the middle of the air and letting the smooth-hot music lap freely around his body. There was going to be a revolution. Yes.

On principle he made one more try at talking.

"I agree with what you said before," he told Tony. "I guess we agree on what we don't like, but I think maybe we ought to talk over what we *do* like."

Tony couldn't be tricked.

"Well," he said. "One thing Gabriel's right. In a revolution, you know, events have a way of making you in action. I learned that in combat."

"I know all about that but that isn't what I'm asking."

For a second they glared at each other contesting who knew what. Then Tony was distracted by a hand passing him a roach.

He's a tired, battle-done old sailor, and I want to go home. What is this, where am I?

Robert Frank brought them up sharp with one of those quiet voices that edge like steel.

"I have something to say to you. Please do not associate me or my group with your activities. As far as I can see, you are a bunch of juvenile delinquents. You, sir [pointing at Gabriel] are a religious fanatic. Good night."

"Now just a minute, buddy . . ." said Conrad Hurvey, chuckling and wheezing, laying his hand on Frank's arm.

"Withdraw your arm or I promise you I shall break it," said Frank.

"That's cool," said Captain Midnight.

Silence, then an eerie blast on the trumpet. Hurvey took his arm away and made a loud chuckle.

"Some pacifist!" he said.

Robert Frank stopped, and Hector was surprised to see

the man obviously pained by Hurvey's retort. Then he turned, and started to leave. Hector started after him to offer a lift home.

Just then Luther Nixon broke through the basement door, a tape recorder in his hand and a pack of bowling-alley toughs at his back.

"Caught in the act!" he cried. "I've got enough here to send you rats to the chair!"

"That's hip," said Captain Midnight, reaching for his belt buckle.

Violence ensued, churning the smoky air. Hector fell quickly, as if swooning. All about him hovered angels of confusion. Before the cops came, Goose Jefferson pushed through the fray and dragged Hector to safety. Later he watched as Gabriel was put into a patrol car, and, when the cops went back for more, Goose opened the far door of the car and wafted him away. As Goose in Hector's car drove his sleeping charges up the Evacuation Route along the Hudson, Gabriel stirred and mumbled in his sleep. When they turned through the college gates and headed past the ghostly drill field, he burst out swearing. "God-dammit I *believe* in the collective unconscious! *I believe in it!*"

Chapter 6

At four the next Monday, Hector Bloom left his Greek Tragedy class taught by Dr Richard Calvin and walked across the campus. Official Winter had stripped the trees bare, but no real cold had come and only enough snow to turn the ground to mud. *Due to maniac testing; southern & northern hemispheres reversed; Panama establishes protectorate over North America.* As he walked, an orange slash of sun tore the cloud-solid sky, and the slash leaped out at Hector, reflected in the flat glass surfaces of new cell buildings. Orange shards of glass rained down upon Hector's ears & brain. As he reeled onwards, students & teachers were not afraid to greet him and tell him what a fine game he had played on Saturday. Some fell into step and walked a few paces alongside him, falling away in his wake with ominous shakings of their cropped heads.

Hector went down into the gym and stoked the furnace for Gabriel. He had trouble shoveling the coal through the

47

opening, and much of it spilled on the floor. Finally he lurched up the stairs and sat on the edge of his bed. Time passed. He wondered if he would rise again. *A message must come from the brain. But where does it come from, and why should it?* His illness often took this form. Time passing; nothing connected.

Hector walked upstairs, and through the fragrant locker-room. Coach Bullion spied him and clapped him heartily on the arm. "How's my Ace!" But when Hector's blank eyes were turned to him, he moaned, "Oh no!" and seized Hector and shook him violently. While Coach Bullion ran for help, Hector wandered past the equipment cage where he would have drawn his practice uniform, up the iron stairs and out the door. As he drove away he passed some team-mates sauntering down for practice; they waved their arms and he blew a toot.

He drove to a street in the college town between the house where Olive lived and the school where she taught dancing. He parked his car under an oak which did not cover him at all and waited till he saw her coming. She came walking along rapidly, her long legs moving her to some marvelous secret purpose.

Then she saw him and he could see how pleased she was.

But would she get into the car? She really shouldn't've: there was supper to be made, didn't he know? She walked gingerly away, while Hector followed her gently with the car in reverse. All at once she gave a little squeal and leaped in.

"Where are you going?"

"To the woods!"

"No, it's too cold."

"To our cottage small by a waterfall."

"No, I don't want to. Please, Hector. . . ."

At a red light she came near and kissed him, filling him up so close and sudden he could hardly breathe. She drew away abruptly.

"Something the matter?"

"Let's just drive, drive. . . ."

It was nearly dark and she lay her head on his shoulder while he drove the bumpy back roads. They had talked many words before but never the right words that might have brought them close beyond suspense: and for once Hector did not want to stop either but to drive on & on never stopping with her head on his shoulder.

They ended having coffee at a drive-in restaurant thirty-two miles from the University. The drive-in was built like an igloo in white stucco to look cool in the summertime, and lit by bare electric bulbs which threw yellow over the inner row but not the back row beyond the drive where cars circled. There were not many cars, yet Hector chose a space directly in back of the building in the dark row up against a rank of fir trees. A drain-faced girl in shiny blue slacks and a mackinaw came into their headlight beams, took the order quickly as she could, and labored cranking her hips back toward the pool of light and the clacking, whining music.

Olive wore black stockings, tempting Hector to spread his hand on her sexy knee. Still they were tense. They fell into separate reveries, staring vacantly into their private wombs of coffee.

"Time to go home?" he asked.

"I suppose so."

"Or do you still think of it as home?"

"I guess I just don't feel like talking. I like it, Hector, today I mean, just being near you without anything happening."

"Playing safe?"

"No. No." With each No she shook her head solemnly from side to side, her eyes so wide he could see the whites all around. She meant it to be loving, the way she looked at him all solemn, but he didn't believe in her sadness. Was she trying to think he could never understand? He felt hopelessly, hopelessly trapped, because he did understand and was irritated, and each irritation seemed only to prove his nonunderstanding. He thought, *How she enjoys it, walking her mind back & forth in some saintly nunnery!* He grabbed her roughly in his arms, but she returned his kiss pensive and wide-eyed and he thrust her roughly away.

He was beginning to see the point they had reached, the point from which there is no going back and no going forward except by a long, daring leap. But she could always make a simple sidestep and drop straight away from the path. She wanted him well enough, as a lover. Love itself was something else. There was too much pleasure in love, too many scenes, too much pain, and always in the end the risk that she might be left nowhere, going top speed either with him or without him but moving with dreadful rapidity straight away from the old known things she might hold onto. She was a professor's wife and she had her home and her things in it and her professor gave her more things, definite things, and she was, after all, married to the brightest most successful now of professors and she the brightest most feminine of wives, and he was older and wiser and took care of her and told her what to do. And her dancing group, too: she could soar, glide, prance, jump & stretch & leap right out of herself, because that's what it really was, and her husband smiling his knowing unintrusive smile to take her home when she was through. Hector she loved as one quick animal loves another, but her husband knew and Hector didn't know at all. Hector knew every inch of her and how she felt every moment, and all this her husband never bothered with and took for granted; but her husband knew who they were and what was right for them, while sweet Hector had to make it up as he went along. Oh he made it up beautifully, and she loved him, but she was her husband's wife.

She laughed, snapping his thoughts in two. She put a playful punch to his stomach.

"We're really duelling now, aren't we?" she said, pretending to wrestle with him.

"And who's winning?" he asked, letting her get a hold on him.

She clapped her hands over his eyes.

"Hector, what do you want of me?"

"I don't know," he said, adding lamely, "I don't know what you mean."

"I knew you'd say that," she said. They sat without moving.

She kissed him, still keeping his eyes covered, then pulled his head down into her lap and stroked his hair.

"You're wrong, you're wrong," he murmured. He knew nothing to say.

He wished he could fall asleep. "Hector," Olive whispered, tensing. "That same car has been passing."

He sat upright. A black Cadillac passed in front of them, circled, passed twice, three times. There was a knocking at the window. Hector rolled the window down and saw in the dark a pair of slit eyes, slack lips, hair long on the sides flat on top: a face not adding up into a face, a man not put together into a man, a youth holding intact the parts of youth until he fell suddenly apart at thirty-five.

"Ya in ah space, mistuh."

"What did you say?"

"Yin ah space, move yuh cah."

Hector got out of the car and stood elaborately facing the youth, Hector quite obviously taller and more powerful.

"Ya gunna move?"

"Why is it important to you?"

The mouth now stiffened into hatred. A faint click . . . and Hector saw a knife blade slip from the right hand held belly-high.

"Do you stab people for asking questions?" Hector's legs tensed, ready to spring back. For the first time he was aware of the noise the Cadillac made, idling in the driveway behind him.

A flood of light poured across them as another car swung into the areaway. The knife retracted.

"Ats right, wise guy."

The youth walked past him and away without the slightest sign of fear. He was insane. Hector, for his part, was trembling as he heard the Cadillac screech around the circle and leave rubber as it shot from the drive back onto the highway. He knew that face . . . from the bowling alley. And elsewhere.

Olive said, "Wasn't that funny? He really thought he was going to scare you with his little knife!" She giggled comfortably, mussed him and rubbed his stomach as he turned the ignition and started up his car, he all the time seeing on the screen of his mind the pale glint from that eye-slit.

"I think they just go around looking for trouble but if you don't give them trouble back they're bored with you and go looking for someone else," Olive said. "Unless you're a woman alone. It's different when you're a woman. You get scared."

"You're scared of a lot of things," Hector said.

"Yes, I am."

Hector drove slowly up a winding side road. "I better take you back," he said.

He felt her tense under his hand, twist around.

"Hector, I think it's that car following us."

"There's something following you, but it's no car."

"Yes it is, *it is!*"

A narrow beam of light shot through his back window, probing for his rearview mirror, hitting it, ripping splinters of light into his eyes. It was the Cadillac, trying to edge beside him now, six men shouting.

He floored his accelerator, his tires yelping as they jerked from the road. Because it was four years old, too old for the good of the country, the automatic transmission bucked, and that one buck was enough for the faster Caddy to jump right back on his bumper. Hector pushed his mirror down and stuck to the middle of the road, blocking so the Caddy couldn't pull up beside him. They played tag for a few miles of country road, Hector holding tight on the curves and opening up space which the heavier car got back as soon as the road straightened. Olive locked all the doors and held whitely to the dashboard.

"Hector, Hector, Hector . . . ," she whimpered.

After three quick miles they whipped through some rapid turns, raced over a hill and into a valley where the road bore straight down on the glowing gut of a great superhighway, which tore luminescent and buzzing through a fertile stretch of truck farms. The Cadillac lost ground on the turns, but every time the road straightened it came right up again and they heard the high steady blare of its horn, manic and *not-to-be-denied, as they say in the sportspages.*

The road made a sudden blind twist, swinging parallel to the highway, and as Hector took the curve he just missed hitting a car speeding in the opposite direction. Before he could get back in the middle the Cadillac jumped up beside him, and he heard their screams mixed with Olive's, saw the magic knife blade flashing. They were forcing him off the road; he heard his tires crunching gravel; in a moment they would bring him to a stop. Without thinking he went for the desperation play: wrenched his wheel sharply to the right and rode jolting across the cabbage patch for the main highway. The steering wheel twisted in & out of control as the car hit the cabbages and slid into the ditches, taking all of Hector's attention so that he lost sight of the Cadillac and feared every second he might jolt loose from the gas pedal and stall there trapped & helpless in the middle of nowhere. At the edge of the highway ran a drainage ditch, and stumpily he pulled the car around until he hit the ditch perpendicular. His front wheels bumped once and got across, but the back wheels stuck on the edge of the ditch and spun and spun and spun *god damn!* till he dropped the lever in low, then shot up and fell back and spun again and again and again and again, while their car was suddenly flooded with light and the Cadillac bore down *Christ!* out of control too slammed into them and knocked them free.

Hector tore down the superhighway at top speed—speedometer stuck at 100—looking for an exit. Olive lay back limply. But there was no exit, and within three minutes the probing light beam came again and the Cadillac was with them, this time with buddies, hot rods, souped-up fliers of the night. More shouts, gleams, horns. Hector gained a few minutes' grace weaving madly back and forth through the three lanes and onto the shoulder, even climbing for an instant the island in the middle. But it couldn't be long now: he heard screams of readiness, howling laughter. *The hunters*. He swerved cunningly around two neutral cars frightened and pulling fast for the side of the road, then feinted and shot through the gap where the chasers might have boxed him. As he bounced off their fenders, his lights caught the sign: EXIT 45 100 YARDS, and once more he whipped the steering wheel, entered the curving ramp on two wheels, his enemies strung behind him like a foxtail. It was too much—in a few seconds he would be back on a small road again and there were many, *oh so many*. He had to take a terrible chance before he got to the end of the ramp: and before he knew it he had jumped the car across the concrete divider and was zipping up the wrong side of the cloverleaf, where cars were supposed to head down. Then one *was* starting down: he sailed free with just enough room for the Caddy to squeeze in behind him. A second later they heard the pile-up crash, but the Cadillac stopped for no friends.

The Cadillac cruisers came all by themselves now with Hector holding them off, keeping steadily to the middle as the road turned and mounted. Sooner or later they must come to a town and people, he was thinking; *either that or a dead-end stopping place*. They had come onto a plateau and were twisting high above the Hudson River, threading the tops of high cliffs, held back only by strings of cable from the mass of white water lying slow and deep beneath the moon. *If they haven't shot yet, they aren't going to shoot*, thought Hector. He almost relaxed. He was conscious of the dead whiteness which washed up to him from so far and washed all color from his brain.

Without warning the Caddy made a desperate lunge to

cut him off. Hector slammed on the brakes, and 1/10 of a second later the Caddy braked. They skidded to a long, trembling stop, Olive pushing frantic against the dashboard, and as their car gently pierced and gently clung to the webbing, they saw the Cadillac dangle for a moment, all crawling inside, then pitch downward, end over end over end, cleaving the water with a silver splash.

They were escaped and alone. Hector stopped not far down the road and opened doors and windows to the odor of dense wet pine trees. He took a pinecone in his hand and squeezed it hard, threw it deep into the rattling woods. Olive stretched on the seat and lay sobbing, then gasping, laughing, and for a long time silent: silent safe alive & young. They knew it. She got out of the car and walked and felt the sod suck firmly at the heels of her shoes. She could have danced, her body was so full. She sat on the seat and took off her shoes and stockings and coat, and with her full skirt blooming ran up and down the road, leaping and spinning in gorgeous arabesques and pirouettes. She danced into the mud and held it with her feet, went up on her toes and pirouetted gracefully backwards and forwards around the delighted Hector, her arms beckoning him to a form he did not know.

She was beckoning him to something, but he did not know.

"Don't let me stand here like an ox!" he cried, and she leapt to him, threw her arms round his waist and hugged him hard, flat-footed—he was astonished at her strength—hugged with all the violence her terror had not spent.

He did what he could. He picked her off the ground and held her face up to his.

"My knight on a white horse," she laughed.

She kissed him and he swung her round and round in his bewilderment, while she screamed with pleasure and he made not a sound.

In a moment they stood quiet. Hector watched her in trancelike dignity: his own deep energy had come when needed and burnt itself away. From his far remove he was still not ready to believe that he could act through volition. He was ready, that's all he was—ready for the next happening.

But Olive knew how utterly alone they were, and how free. She came to him, and he would have lain right down with her, right there in the woods.

"It's too wet, it's cold," she said. "Let's go back in. I like it here, don't you?"

He held her gently on the seat of his automobile. They lay for a long time just breathing together and warming each other and feeling themselves so near. *Olive, Olive,* thought Hector. He had no desire but to lie there indefinitely in her warmth and his quiet. "Oh yes!" she said, and he came to her from afar, with open eyes to her closed ones. He was beginning to feel appalled at her passion—would she not try to contact him, to come where he was, to be with him & of him?

No, she went ahead. He could feel his life flowing into her, surrounding her in gain, steady gain, and all so simple that the final pain came as a shock, as a tree stabbing deep and branching, her pride full of Hector, who came back to flesh with a mighty, head-thrown roar of love, as his seed stampeding shot the gap to immortality.

She nestled to him, nestled to him, clung avidly to her strong man while he lay unknown to her: sticky, sweaty, exhausted in every resource and close to tears. Whatever there had been was not enough. He had never in his life felt so alone.

Too many things had happened; tomorrow he would feel refreshed, & glad for this. In his last thought before he curled into the grip of deepest sleep, he yearned for the clean true feel of a basketball.

Chapter 7

⟶ A bright Sunday in February, hard winter sun beating into blue snow, and Hector Bloom laid out in his little room near the boilers, sulking beneath his sheets drawn up in a tent.

He had not seen much of Olive; he sensed her slipping from him, treasuring up her emotions in long spaces of silence and chastity. She had come the last time the night before his midyear exams began, come in darkness and gone over his body carefully, perhaps memorizing; smoothing and nipping as though he were a fine statue she had magically lifted from the museum and must love completely before the dawn guards came.

"Why?" he had asked her. "Why not? Why don't I see you more?"

"Oh Hector," she said. "I'm worried. Morton has enough information on you to . . . to . . . to send you. . . ."

"Then he knows!"

"No, he doesn't know. About us, you mean. He doesn't know anything. He doesn't want to know things like that."

"Then tell him!"

"I can't."

"You must tell him, you've got to!" As she fell silent, Hector grew obsessed. "Look how you are! Can you keep on this way?"

She wept a little; shrugged away from his touch.

But Hector couldn't stop. "You still sleep with him don't you? How could you?"

"You don't know how it is."

"How is it? Tell me. Here I am: tell me."

But she was gone.

Hector's basketball suffered. His diffusion was worse than ever. Yet since there was never a time when he couldn't score, the experts still saw an All-American when they looked at him. The experts are always behind. From outside Hector they couldn't know the incompleteness, the ball just off his fingers instead of inside them, the step missed and the last-second grab, the lunge, the slap. More than ever he was impatient on defense. Who had time to follow petty maneuverings? He did not dribble much himself, nor did he make excessive fakings. The clean, straightforward move developing into an unexpected countermove: and he was up in the air all by himself alone with the ball drifting from the ends of his fingers. But he was shooting a trifle less and missing a trifle more. The team knew—he was losing touch with them. Goose knew, and waited, and strained a thigh muscle trying to make up the difference.

Something had to happen, he knew that. The real thing—but wherever he went it was wrong. He feared his own exaltation. Since his days of adolescence, he had not known what it meant not to be a star. Life wasn't like that. But he didn't care what life was like. *I'll do more than survive!* he swore.

Now Gabriel was in the room. "Let's go, man! Yes!" He swept the white pure tent away and beamed a flashlight into Hector's hidden eyes.

"Yes Yes Yes Yes Yes!"

He got Hector into the car, nonsmiling but willing, and they set off together for Long Island to crash the sixty-fifth birthday extravaganza of Olive's father, the celebrated Moses Mandel.

As a Major General, Moses Mandel had directed the American supply system during World War II. After the war he had retired from the service, and was by now Chairman of a munitions plant the biggest in the world next to Krupp: Dewdrop Ltd. The party was taking place on his estate, whence flocked the cream of the military, industrial and media worlds to honor him. Even great artists like the Valentine brothers were there. Indeed, the estate that Sunday was an Arcadia of celebrities, for Moses Mandel's entire lawn—vast enough to contain multiple polo fields— had been enclosed in the latest achievement in bomb protectors: a huge puncture-proof transparent fiber-tight plastic bubble, within which the star-spangled guests capered and chattered, coatless, warm and merry as a summer day. This dome was only a scaled-down model of the great hydrogen-proof dome that Dewdrop Ltd was in the process of erecting over the whole of New York City, and whose replicas would eventually enclose every on-the-ball American metropolis. The dome posed a problem for Hector and Gabriel, however, as the only way they could enter the lawn was by means of a narrow underground passageway closely guarded by security agents. Fortunately Moses

Mandel himself happened to be standing for a moment in the entrance, giving last-minute instructions to his Senator, and instantly seized Hector by the arm.

"Ah, the basketball star!" he said. "I recognize you. Well well well well well, we have much to talk about. I often watch you on TV, you know that? I saw you just the other day."

He kept pumping Hector's hand as he led him out of the tunnel and up onto the lawn, where people began to pile up and clutter about them. Moses Mandel kept one soft hand in the middle of Hector's back, by which he pushed him up to Morton Solomon. Morton looked surprised and amused, and behind him Olive turned, her hair swept up in a glistening coil, leaving her ears white as shells and face smooth-creamed as an Egyptian queen's, her arms white, her bosom white in a silk dress cut low and clinging in a halter round her slender neck. Her lips parted and her eyes gleamed; she was laughing.

"Morton, I've brought you one of your young men I always hear you talk about." Moses was always bringing people exactly what they didn't need. On Hector, for example, he forced a raw pineapple full of tomato juice, tequila, and black Asian rum.

Moses Mandel went on pumping pumping, his hand in Hector's like a little girl's. He put his incredibly drooped and crisscrossed face close up to Hector's, so that Hector could smell his potent breath. "You know, we old men, that's all we have to do, sit and watch the young athletes on TV. My generation ruined their lives, and yours won't do any better.

"I mean yours too, Morton, you won't get away from this! Your generation and mine are the same. We thought we knew the answers, but we didn't even know the questions."

He snatched up a martini from a passing tray, and with drink held in three fingers pointed the fourth straight between Morton's eyes. Morton made a deprecating gesture, brushing away an imaginary spider dangling from the end of his nose. "Don't brush, don't brush!" Moses shouted. "You *know* what I mean!" On the word "know," he stabbed Morton in the diaphragm, splashing a thimble of gin on Morton's vest.

His clutch had moved to Hector's upper arm. "But you must meet my wife, you must meet my wife. Julia! JULIA!" he shouted, as though his wife were on the outside of the bubble.

But from quite near, a distinguished-looking lady from the most aristocratic of cigarette packages slipped past the editors of America's two largest weeklies, by dint of an exceptionally broad and handsome pair of shoulders. Hector recognized Lady Julia Mandel, Moses' English noblewife. The woman had apparently not yet greeted her daughter and son-in-law, and as she offered them her cheek, Hector was startled by her forklike eyes and stern narrow jaw-line, in which he saw a flash of Olive with her arteries hardened. Lady Julia gave Hector her hand as an equal, and he was shocked to see, as she shook it one brief shake, an almost coquettish smile on her lips.

"Julia, Julia, what do you think? This is Hector Bloom, the Jewish basketball star!"

"That's right," said Olive, "he was circumsized in a gala half-time ceremony!"

The glassed-in laughter reverberated hysterically the length of the lawn.

"Oh I'm so exhausted these days," Lady Julia exclaimed, and several others said the same thing. It was hard to tell who had said it first. Hector tried a brandy sour.

Tony Valentine and Billy-Gene were close by—Hector had a glimpse of Billy-Gene camping in the most exotic silken clothes he had ever seen. The pants were violet, the shirt rose, and on his head a huge rose-violet-orange silk turban.

Richard Calvin was there, listening to Lady Julia and to Morton. Lady Julia was not merely Moses' wife; she was an established literary critic, whose study, *God is Love* or *D. H. Lawrence Supervised*, had made a stir within discreet circles. Richard looked sleepy, as though he were about to tumble headfirst into his martini glass.

Suddenly Richard was confronted by Tony Valentine standing hands on hips.

"All right Richard," Tony said, glancing sideways at Hector, "here's what I want you to do. If someone should come up and hit you, first I want you to throw your drink in his face. Then bring your leg up and knee him in the balls. Have you got that?"

"Yes."

"Will you do it?"

"Of course not."

"You know, I knew you wouldn't."

Tony vanished. Trying to follow him, Hector ran into Gabriel with his girl Claudine. She was high; her little face was flush with beads of sweat. While Gabriel and Hector leaned against the side of the bubble, she burbled fluidly about the new South American liberator.

". . . well, you know, it was wonderful, I mean all those people cheering and shouting '*Muerte! Muerte!*' All together and you know, like so *Latiny* and everything, I just never felt like that before. Personally, I mean. And then the Leader stood up in his People's Uniform and asked for silence, and asked the people for mercy, that he would spare these Enemies of the State for the time being . . . and anyway everyone fell you know to cheering again like I mean in *rhythm*, and God it was so *great!* I just got carried away. I was totally *absorbed*. You know what I mean? I mean *I* didn't exist anymore, it was just *us, us, us.* . . ."

As Hector slid away along the curved wall, she was still shaking her head in disbelievement. "*So great, so great, so great.* . . ."

Another crowd was collecting by the mammoth barbecue pit, where a covey of Polynesian servants were turning a dozen oxen on spits. Lady Julia had collared Billy-Gene Valentine and in a voice cultured as a quarterly was lecturing him on his morals & poetry. Lady Julia had written a definitive essay on the younger poets and was galled to see their number one "spokesman" camping around her lawn trying to seduce people, just as as though he didn't know what she thought of him.

"I am a Seraph of naked beauty," Billy-Gene explained. "There is nothing but love in my heart. I follow my erection, wherever it may lead."

"That's not love," retorted Lady Julia, "but simple selfishness and irresponsibility."

"Oh dear," moaned Billy-Gene. "She's after my responsibles."

"Your immaturity is disheartening," said Lady Julia. "We were discussing what you refer to as your poetry. Since you admit that your compositions contain nothing but subconscious ravings, how can we possibly call them Art?"

"Art? Art who? Don't call them Art, dear lady, call a taxi. Call the fire department, call the national guard, call a moratorium, call a general strike, call a Communist, call your congressman, call a doctor and *plunge* yourself into therapy."

"I can see that serious discussion is impossible!"

"Dry-ice therapy," Billy-Gene added.

"Look, young man, aren't you being a bit simpleminded? Isn't it just an easy way out to see everything in terms of black & white? Yes, I know, you and your friends are angels, and the rest of us devils plotting to destroy you. But isn't life always so much more *complex?* As a literary person aren't you obliged to offer some value which might make life meaningful for your readers?"

"Why madam," replied Billy-Gene, "you are speaking to the inventor of heroin vaseline."

"Arrant nonsense!" Lady Julia stamped her foot.

"Precisely," said Billy-Gene. "And that's only my most modest value."

"You have no value! WHY DON'T YOU GET A JOB!"

"I *have* a job, dear lady. You see me dressed in the festive garb of messenger boy to the Gods. I get paid in cosmic juicejolts to tell you this: death draweth nigh. You're going to die, lady, die die-dee-eye-die die! Slush! The Ice Bomb gets you! Your eyes are fringed with pearls of ice! Charming fleshflies buzz about in your jewelry. No outlet for your electric corset I'm afraid. The ice breeds maggots of envy lust greed and indigestion. You run from pole to pole, dripping crusted cunt and vomit-running nose as you weep across the ice. Ah, what have you done to the grass, lady? It's freezing tragic, who will save you? From the depths of your being comes a well-disciplined groan. Alas, the God of Discipline is busy at toil; he throws you a shroud to suck. But do not despair! There is one who heeds your cry! The heavens open and a golden cloud appears. And from the cloud *I* issue forth, *I*, Queen of the Universe! Five for a dollar! Light me up like a Christmas candle and *watch me burn!*"

Billy-Gene jumped elegantly atop a turning ox, and kept his balance by jumping through a wild Pomeranian goat-dance, all the time chanting sacred prophecies, most of them in Pomeranian.

"OFF WITH HIS BALLS!" bellowed Lady Julia.

"Oh, goody!" said Billy-Gene. He sailed from his ox, landing gracefully not three yards in front of her. He stood calmly while a hush fell over the congregation.

Lady Julia was shocked at her loss of control. She drew herself together now and spoke in a voice heavy with the dignity of centuries of uranium:

"Do you really think that was necessary, young man? Is that your idea of 'naked beauty'?"

Billy-Gene bowed low, and, with an even heavier dignity, the dignity of centuries of fools, took down his violet pants. He stood there in self-possession, swinging his testicles to and fro as a brace of security agents converged on him.

Lady Julia's veins were dancing, but as a point of ancient honor she did not look away until the offender was hauled from her presence, the agents businesslike and professionally oblivious to the fact that Tony Valentine was converging on *them*, just as he had converged on the Sunday-school picnic in his movie *Aces Wild*.

A shadow had fallen across the bubbled lawn. People were swirling rapidly, like drowning ants. From inside his glass Hector heard Morton Solomon report the latest news. Our observers had installed a native General on the Island, who would restore property to its rightful owners and bring democracy at last. Solomon spoke with his habitual irony, which Richard Calvin chose to ignore. "But face it," he cried: "Evil is real! People are bestial! Can't you understand that?"

"Perfectly," Solomon assured him. "Nevertheless, some governments are less evil than others."

Their voices were submerged in the thousand violins of the Maraschino Strings, more or less simultaneously embarking on Handel's *Water Music*, from a huge Tutankhamenian bark stationed in a lily pond. People put small sandwiches into their mouths, and here and there a drunk lay down behind a bush and pressed his face into the damp blue grass.

Moses Mandel reappeared at Hector's side and drew him through a group of admirals and society reporters up a flight of fiberglass steps between looming pillars and into the house itself, where he found himself alone with Moses in a mahogany-paneled study. One end of the study opened out into a picture window overlooking the sweep of the lawn, whereon the guests were deployed. Hector saw Olive below, chatting with a man in cap and gown. Moses blew her a kiss from his slabbed lips, but she turned away in disgust.

At once Moses strode to the alabaster fireplace, where he noisily dragged great logs across the hearthstone and set about lighting a fire, all the time shouting to his wife as though she were in the room. "Julia!" Huffing and puffing. "Look at me, Julia, I'm making a fire!" A piece of bark tore his pants leg. "Julia, are you tired? There's nothing like a fire to warm your bones and make you feel at home. Hand me that big one, will you young fella? Julia, do you like it now? Julia, *are you happy?*"

"Just ignore him," said Lady Julia to Hector as she entered the room.

"Julia!" Moses rushed to her, grasping futilely for her hands. "Julia, you're not happy with me. Why aren't we happy? Why are we never happy anymore?" (He was trying to kiss her folded neck, to fondle her breast.)

"Moses, go away!"

Moses turned to Hector with a philosophic shrug. "You see, love doesn't last, young man. Julia, tell me darling, why don't you love me? Is it because I'm old? Is it because I'm old and ugly?"

"It's because you talk too much," snapped Lady Julia. As she marched out of the room she threw Hector a long-practiced smile: isn't-he-silly-it's-all-in-fun.

Moses ran after her and Hector could hear him pleading, whining, why don't you love me why don't you love me? and her whisper harsh with anger and embarrassment.

Holding tightly to his cognac glass, Hector made an effort to look out the window. The dying sun was sliding dense purple shafts into the plastic bowl, and the guests moved heavily, as though walking on the bottom of the ocean. Like seaweed dust, fumes of darkness rose from the ground to snatch at their ankles.

Moses came back and drew Hector by the elbow into a corner, as if to conspire.

"Can you swim, young man?"

"Not a stroke," Hector confessed.

"Excellent then!" the old man cried. "Why don't you wait until everyone leaves, and then we'll all go in for a nice moonlight swim! You'd like that, wouldn't you? Just our family group, Olive too! You like Olive, don't you? You know you and I must get to know one another. Tell me, what is your deepest desire? Yes, you do admire my daughter. Isn't she wonderful. I tell you frankly, frankly Hector . . . [he paused, and looked up with face so wise and Socratic-sad that he might be imparting his deepest secret] . . . that girl is the only reason I go on living."

Moses took Hector on a tour of the room. "This tapestry Julia and I got when we were in Pakistan. *Fright*fully expensive. You wouldn't believe how much it costs. The little figurine over here is expensive too. This is the kind of thing I once swore we'd never spend money on. Och! At your age! At your age. . . . But when you get older it doesn't mean the same thing to you. You'll find out! It makes my wife happy to have beautiful things, so we buy them. Just like that! Do you think I know? Do you think I care? Listen: in five, ten years I'll be dead and this is all my grandchildren will remember of me. You'll be here. They'll tell you our grandfather was the funny old man who bought this junk.

"Here's Julia's family coat of arms. And this on the wall is from a very great general I had better not name. Ugly, isn't it? And the rug you're standing on I got from the President when I retired. Turkish, I won't even begin to tell you what it must have cost him.

"This painting, ech, if I should tell you what this one sold for! But it's gorgeous, isn't it? Look at this painting, Hector. That's no copy, Hector, it's an original. The man who painted this is one of the greatest men I know. No, I'll put it this way [he grabbed Hector's chest and looked piercingly up into his eyes]: he's the one great man I know. The one great man I know. Do you understand that, Hector? In all my generation the one great man!"

"I think so," Hector said.

"I think you do. [He looked away content.] Now the

man who painted this, whatsisname, insisted that Julia, no one else but Julia must own this painting. So what could I do? I bought it!"

He burst out in bitter laughter.

"Do you think I know why? I just bought it, that's all. Hector do we ever know why we do things? We're afraid to die—that's all it is, Hector, we're afraid to die!"

Moses took Hector for a walk in an enclosed garden behind the house. He was telling Hector one of the stories of his life. He had been a witness to every human pain. Born in a dreary Russian *stetl* where men struggled through the mud, at ten he came to New York to be a little *yeshivah bucher* while his father peddled 2nd-hand clothes from a pushcart on the Lower East Side. Then he became "a young idealist" at City College. "We sat on the steps at night and talked the most marvelous ideas in the world—everyone! There was no need for realism. What was reality but tenements and trash! We were free to dream the most stupendous dreams ever dreamt: we really dreamt *America!* And we were right! Only we were wrong about ourselves.

"What a long way we've come in this century, Hector! And how much we've given up! You think these things are easy. Yes, easy to you, but you're young, you don't know! You think it's easy to have a daughter like Olive? I didn't like Morton Solomon at first, but now . . . we get along. Suppose my children did me the trick of refusing my money—who would be the victim? Me! Because otherwise my life would be ludicrously empty. The only way they can keep their self-respect is to take it with contempt. And they're right! I understand. I have a sister I never see. You know why I never see her? Because she's filthy, Hector, coming from California you never saw such filth. The woman doesn't know what it means to clean her house or even take a bath. She's poor and vulgar and Hector a young man in your class wouldn't spend five minutes of your time of day with her. But *she* thinks I'm a rich prick and a traitor to the working class. Writes my wife letters threatening to kidnap Olive and take her to China. You think that's easy to take?

"Hector! Julia's brother committed suicide! Julia will be haunted the rest of her life. Just think of that. Did you know that? No, of course you don't, no one does. They all think he was bitten by a dog. Picture this, Hector, one of the richest young men in Europe, fabulously rich, all the talent and education in the world, graduated from Oxford, rich beautiful American wife (not Jewish either), three beautiful children, beautiful estate in the country and winters on the Riviera, went into the garage one day and gassed himself. No reason, don't ask me. I don't even know why I'm telling you these things. It's none of your affair, really. But you want to know, don't you, Hector? You like my daughter, don't you? Don't answer! I know! You think I don't know?

"Hector, in my own lifetime so many of the faiths and beliefs and everything men held most sacred failed dismally, dismally, tragically when they came into realization. Imagine this, Hector, we believed people could be held together! We believed in rational economies! We believed in families, in fathers and sons even! And then so much that I believed in personally was built up out of no real knowledge of the nature of life or how people lived inside. Abysmal ignorance, that's what I built my views on. I was young. But every school child knows better now! I see these young kids; I know! I'm drunk now, that's why I'm telling you this. Don't ask me what became of my own father!

"Life is a farce, Hector, a ghastly farce. Don't smile at

me. You think this is sophomoric wisdom, but it isn't, believe me. Look at my face, Hector: is this the face of a sophomore? [*He knows it isn't, he's using it, old sad ugly face in layers of flesh.*] Hector you wouldn't believe me how little I have to believe in. My grandchildren aren't born yet, and already I don't believe in them, even them!

"I'm against things, that's the best I can do. I hate totalitarianism, I fear men in power, I live in dread fear of the absolute truth. Negative virtues, but all I have. Love? Who can love a man of so little faith? What promise in yellow teeth and bloated flesh? Could *you* love me, Hector? Bah, don't answer!"

Thought Hector, *I could; I do.*

"Hector, I want to do something I've never done in my whole life. I'm going to take a frightful chance with you, Hector, I'm going to . . ." and here he broke off and they walked on in silence.

"Hector! What are you going to do with yourself!"

"I'd like to go in and get near the fire," Hector said.

Around the fire stood Morton and Richard Calvin and Lady Julia, drinking martinis and continuing their political discussion. Standing with his back to the doorway was a short man with grey head cocked and listening whom Hector recognized as Robert Frank, the pacifist. Hector wanted to say hello, but before he could the circle was distracted by Tony Valentine. Sporting a puffed discolored eye and a trickle of blood along his lip, Tony went straight for Richard Calvin and violently seized upon him. Clearly there was some terrible crisis.

"Look Richard, will you do this much? Will you splash the drink in his eyes? Then all you have to do is hit him once or twice in the stomach!"

"But Tony, I don't always carry a drink!"

Tony spat contemptuously on Richard Calvin's shoe, and, lowering his shoulder, crashed through the glass doors to the garden, just as the security agents came charging through the room after him.

"General Mandel, I would like to talk to you about a matter of great importance."

It was Robert Frank speaking, and once again Hector was startled by the formal clarity of his voice. In a carefully controlled tone, Robert Frank was telling Moses how impressed he was by the luxury of the party, the house and grounds, the abundance of food and pleasure.

"General Mandel, I believe I owe my invitation here to the fact that both you and I are directors of the International Children's Fund. But it's been years since I've seen you. Do you remember me, Moses?"

"*Veh is mir!* Bobby Frank!" It seemed they had known each other on the Lower East Side, where Frank had come to work at the Henry Street Settlement, trying his best to be a good young Quaker and in fact keeping his faith all the way to the time of Hitler. Moses was acting gratified, though it seemed to Hector there was a new wariness about him, as if he wanted to be pleased with himself and then abruptly break away. But Frank held Moses fast with his intense, direct manner.

"You see," Frank said, "I'm puzzled by the contradiction."

"Ah Bobby, you haven't changed a bit—still puzzled by contradictions."

"But in your case, General Mandel, the contradiction is extreme. On one hand you fight the Nazis, you go in for philanthropy, you like to give people things and make them grateful. On the other, you own the lion's share of our country's largest weapons producer. So you pay your charity with blood money you win in the crap game of annihilation. How do you keep it up, Moses? How do you live with yourself split in half? I urge you as an old friend and a fellow human being—come over to the side of peace and use your influence for a general disarmament!"

Moses' eyebrows went up in a pantomime of innocence. "But haven't you heard? I'm already on your side! Just last month I was appointed to the President's Special Committee on Arms Reduction!"

Robert Frank clenched his square jaw and Hector saw his underlip tighten to a white line. The man was genuinely surprised, and struggled hard against some immense violence within himself. Hector saw, too, how Richard Calvin restrained his laughter.

"How could you . . ." Frank muttered, then drew even more irrationally upright than before, more upright than anyone would have thought his ordinary stockiness could permit, and said, "How could you be so evil?"

Hector saw Lady Julia start up at the bluntness, but Moses relaxed, *like a real pro*. "You know, Bobby," Moses said, "you were such a fine person as a young man—I can see you still are—a fine person, a good person, but you'll forgive me maybe for saying you could have been a better student. Your basic economics you had trouble with, Bobby, even then, and that was where the rest of us were all so good.

"No, don't interrupt me, I'll answer your question. I'll give you my philosophy. You see the world don't stay the same, it changes, and if you don't change it goes on without you."

Here he really looked at Frank for the first time.

"OK, so I'm evil. How do I live with myself? Wretchedly! But why stop with me, why specialize? So you want to denounce, denounce, but tell everything or else you don't have the truth. The whole truth I don't mind, believe me, my heart goes out to you. Only I worry you won't have the strength. I know *I* don't have the strength. You see, Bobby, I know these men, I know the President, the Senate, the successful and the fabulously successful of our time, and this is what I have seen, what I have seen in my lifetime. I have seen the most deliberate perversion and abasement and defilation of morality the world has ever known, ever, and on such a scale you can't imagine not even in your wildest dreams. You think I don't know that? You think the others don't know? You think they're stupid? Believe me, Bobby, stupid they're not. They know as well as you, Bobby, but they can't resist, they're corrupt, men have always been corrupt but God with *such power!*—that's what does it, not this crummy food and this chintzy house, *power*, the knowledge that no man can get away from what you do, no one can ignore what you say, what you feel. Think of that! One man, two men, three men: they make up their minds and their words go around the world on electricity. Millions of lives changed with every impulse. And people accept! They never hear different! That's why we're doomed, and when I say doomed believe me I mean doomed far beyond the efforts of insects like you and me to do anything about it. No one escapes, no one! Don't kid yourself.

"Yes, we mighty people, what did you say about us? We're successful, all right successful, that's our crime, successful beyond anything your father or mine could have conceived for a pasha even. Which means we're the ones the others want to be like. But what are we really? We're worse than failures. As failures we might have stood for something.

No, your denouncing I don't mind, but why bother? We're nothing, nothing, pieces of refuse in the filthy gutter. OK, denounce us if you like, but when you're through weep for us, yes weep, weep for us, weep for our poverty, weep for our pettiness, weep because we're everything we wanted to be. Do you know that in our great moments we actually believe what we say! We don't even have the courage to be cynical! Do you think we love ourselves? Bobby what you see is loathing, loathing! Love? Is there such a thing as love? If you don't have it we don't have it either. We got nothing but misery and impotence and hatred. Yes I said impotence! Among the most powerful men on earth! It's nothing new—any harlot could tell you—oh weep for us, that's all we expect, weep weep weep. . . ."

And sure enough, to the disgust of all, Lady Julia was weeping, her nails clawing at her bony face, her broad shoulders heaving like those of the sophomore fullback who's booted away the Homecoming Game. There were snickers of embarrassment. This was the last thing Moses wanted. Doubtless he would have been happy if everyone had laughed, and taken another drink.

Moses Mandel stepped to his wife, and in a voice deliberate as a comedian's pronounced his one clear sentence:

"Julia, why don't you love me?"

A desperate silence.

"Julia????"

"Oh Moses!" She turned to Robert Frank with her coy smile of culture. "You really must forgive my husband. . . ."

"He forgives me, darling. But do *you* forgive me? That's the real question."

"Oh yes then: I forgive you." She walked around him and

77

kissed him mockingly, put her fingers on a roll of his cheek and pinched. "Who couldn't forgive you?"

"You can only forgive someone you don't love. Now I know you don't love me, Julia."

"Moses!" There was last-ditch anger in her tone.

"Moses, my dear, I love you, forgive you, obey & revere you: I am your slave."

She glanced round triumphant.

"Do you love me then? You mean it?"

"Love and adore you, darling, worship you like a god. . . ."

Give a man enough rope, said her charming smile, her pleasing, smirking, aging lips, now set so high. . . .

"AH HA!" Moses shouted. "Now we have answered the first question. Now we have answered the riddle, Why don't you love me? Now what I want to know is:

[and here his face turned grave as a small, small boy's]

"Why don't I love you?"

Robert Frank came up to Hector. "Mr Bloom," he said, "within two weeks we will begin a program of direct action designed to shut down Dewdrop Ltd. I've been told you might join us. The support of any public figure means a great deal."

"One moment, Hector," said Morton Solomon. "Just how do you propose to shut down Dewdrop Ltd, Mr Frank?"

"We will bear witness to the deadly nature of the work there. We will oppose that work with our own bodies if need be. When the workers understand that to do their work is to harm other human beings, they will leave their jobs."

"And how many witness bearers do you have?"

"Potentially we have millions, Dr Solomon. If you will join us, that will make one more."

"But in actual fact you'd be lucky to raise a hundred. Now each Dewdrop factory has about 15,000 employees. That means, let's see . . . each witness will have to come between 150 men and the means by which they feed and clothe their families. Your people must have extraordinary bodies, Mr Frank! Perhaps we should throw them directly in front of the Enemy!"

Robert Frank either could not, or would not, reply to this. Looking most unhappy, he turned again to Hector. "How about it, Mr Bloom?" Seeing his square, plain face already set for defeat, Hector wanted to burst into tears. He reeled, overcome with drink and guilt. He could not face the mockery of Morton Solomon's smile.

"I'm sorry," Hector mumbled. "Don't have the time. . . ."

Robert Frank turned and left. Morton Solomon put his hand on Hector's shoulder and shook his head slowly, smiling grimly down at their shoes. You & I, said the smile, you & I, Hector. *Together we know!*

Though he knew not what they knew, Hector, too, felt sad & old & wise. And tired. Then sad & old & wise Moses Mandel put his hand on Hector's other shoulder and said, "That was right, Hector. You said the only thing you could possibly say. It was so pathetic, so pathetic . . . and you saw that, Hector. Don't worry, don't think twice."

A deep, gasping sigh wrenched its way loose from inside Moses. "Ah, Hector, people are frightfully sad. . . . I never met a man I didn't feel sorry for. Not a man, not one. But tell me then, Hector, why do I hate? Why do I envy? Why must I triumph? Why don't I have more compassion? This business of human beings—it's all so frightfully sad, sad, sad. . . ."

Hector stumbled forward and vomited into the alabaster fireplace.

Night surrounded the dome, stars twinkled through the plastic heaven, and Hector was looking for Olive. Was that she, teetering past the group chattering and flashing their teeth in the dark and wetting their tuxedoes on the grass roasting hot dogs in the oxpit? He raced round the oxpit once, twice, grabbed roasting ladies by the shoulders and peered closely into their faces.

It seemed that no one had left. Most of the people were sitting down now and passing marijuana cigarettes from an abundant store of good leaf supplied for the occasion by Billy-Gene Valentine. Billy-Gene had predicted that marijuana would become absolute among the truly cool, and was doing his best to make the prediction come true. Before long the pungent pot smoke collected under the plastic dome so thick that Hector could hardly see, and breathing for all alike became a throat-tickling brain-reeling delight. Hector had to guide himself about by the glowing sparks of roach-tips in the darkness, and approaching one thick-studded cluster, he was curiously exalted to see an old woman with ears of diamonds pronounce herself Cassandra, and climb atop a huge Ethiopian servant to speak her prophecy. Her voice was strong as a patriarch's, and she spoke not as Homer but Isaiah:

The treacherous dealers have dealt treacherously;
Yea, the treacherous dealers have dealt very treacherously.

Fear, and the pit, and the snare, are upon thee,
O inhabitant of the earth.
And it shall come to pass,
That he who fleeth from the noise of the fear shall fall into
the pit;
And he that cometh up out of the midst of the pit shall be
taken in the snare:
For the windows from on high are open,
And the foundations of the earth do shake.
The earth is utterly broken down,
The earth is clean dissolved,
The earth is moved exceedingly.
The earth shall move to and fro like a drunkard,
And shall be removed like a cottage;
And the transgression thereof shall be heavy upon it;
And it shall fall, and not rise again.

As he listened, Hector found that he had begun to twist
his body and flibber his lips with his fingers, making an un-
dercurrent of babel to the woman's preaching. To snap
himself out of it he snatched a silver tureen of cold chicken
bouillon, and sucked it down in one gulp.

At last he saw Olive, a lorn & lonely woman hung over
the net of a darkened tennis court. He fled to her for love.
When he took her up, however, she turned out to be Gabriel's girl Claudine. Hector set her on her feet and walked
her up & down till she revived, whereupon she murmured
thank you thank you thank you, and standing tippytoe
planted rows of soft wet babykisses on his neck. Just then
Gabriel came charging up.

"Oh my God, oh my God!" shrieked Gabriel. "My God
you should have seen it, where were you baby, you missed

the greatest of the year! Billy-Gene and Tony just spiked the punch with LSD and now the whole bag of stiffs is gonna start hallucinating!"

And it was true. From the other side of the lawn came the bellows and snorts of imaginary hippopotami, the prattle of monkeys, and the leaping thump-thump of merry kangaroos at play. Claudine, however, smiled cunningly.

"Isn't that a bit gauche?" She unfolded her Bennington portable potter's wheel and calmly began to shape a pot.

An imaginary condor flew overhead, clutching in its talons an elderly Arabian diplomat. Its mighty wingspread blotted out the stars, and threw a shadow of remorse across Hector's troubled mind. *Olive*, where was she?

In his haste to pursue her he charged through Claudine's apparatus and ran several yards with his foot encased in clay.

Hector was chasing Olive Solomon through clouds of marijuana smoke. She ran coolly and deliberately, taking good advantage of obstructions offered by fallen and clustered people. *My conquest that I can never win*, he thought, *I'll get her & get her good* (for good?). She turned, and interposed the house between them. He could see her eyes laughing at him through the windows. Olive fled up a hill and through a bath house, emerging in a bathing suit her long legs gleaming as she ran through the night. Her black hair was streaming full of stars. Hector fell down and rolled in a ditch, sat up, got up, didn't know where she was. He tried to tie his shoe, but his shoestring broke so that when he started running he tripped again. He was fast, so much faster than she, and he would catch her, too, if only he knew how.

Perhaps she was on the dance floor—he caught a gleam

of moonlight from her smooth pale shoulder among the packed-in dancers gyrating to the bombular thumpings of the Megaton Maniac & His Hydroheroin Heptet. The Maniac himself stood inverted in front of the group, the first in town to puff his horn inward, sucking & wheezing until with an incredible high note that turned the fruit on Mrs Porter's hat to jelly, he absorbed the horn and stood playing his lungs like an accordion and gasping in the music.

Hector watched the packed dancers carefully, straining to catch another glimpse of his Olive. The dancers were performing a strange dance, each separate by a few inches from the other and anchored legs apart by the heels, twisting the middle body and flapping the toes. *Ah*, thought Hector at first, *that's good, good & simple, they need things simple, put two together and you have a plain old fuck.* Then he saw their elbows tight fists clenched eyes closed and he was seized with horror. No, it was death they danced for, violent lonely death: no lust could make them move so, each closed off from the other squirming isolate fists closed struggling insects in one last orgy of masturbation to supplicate down on themselves the final brutish noise that would spin them loose from their emptiness. Even as he watched, a trap door under the bandstand suddenly opened and swallowed the combo, leaving in its wake a suffocating silence, which blanketed the lawn like gas. The dancers coughed for air, and fell down swooning, leaving Olive standing slender moon-silver like the heart of an onion.

Exerting all the power of his legs and shoulders, Hector pushed through the heavy silence toward Olive. She held out her arms as if to embrace him, but when he drew near, leaped in a light *jeté*, kissed him on the forehead, and flitted away like a hummingbird.

Gradually he gained on her, a pack of people thumping along behind him.

"But I love you!" he cried.

"So touchingly sincere!" she trilled back.

"I can be ironic, too, when I want to!" he shouted, and heard the whole pack behind him break into sarcastic laughter.

Up winding ivory stairs set into a hillside he pursued her. When he got to the top he discovered a dazzling golden swimming pool cut into the night. Olive was bounding silkily on the end of the diving board, her mad laugh mocking him a torrent of crystal. He circled the gleaming pool and climbed out after her.

She leapt once and out of his arms, twice, the diving board vibrating, and then he caught her fast, nearly crushing her.

"Oh Hector," she whined in exasperation, "let me go! Get away from me, you huge boy, you *naïf!*"

His hold melted and she shoved him with all her might. He fell heavily in the water, and felt it sucking him down, cool, pushing back against his struggling, closing over his head thick and fragrant as blood. His tight muscles relaxed, and gladly gave themselves over to the flowing neverending muscles of the water.

When he got to the top of the hill, Gabriel Reuben found Morton Solomon wavering on the edge of the pool. When Morton saw Gabriel he backed away and pointed. Gabriel quickly shed his clothes, plunged in, and straining with all his might brought Hector to the surface.

But Hector's skin was blue, and his face set in a ghastly grin that started tremors in Gabriel's stomach. He put a tentative hand between the broad wet shoulders. Gabriel was scared out of his mind. The great Hector was no longer breathing, and no one knew what to do. . . .

Outside a mighty rainstorm lashed at the dome. Hector heard, and breathed, felt hands and raised one cold eyelid. He saw a shape bent over him, started to lift, then at the murmuring of a few soft words relaxed, and let the hands that had revived him, the silken hands of Billy-Gene Valentine, slowly and dreadfully massage the blood back into his upper body.

The silence had been penetrated now, and all at once exfoliated into a hideous commotion. To Gabriel standing, Billy-Gene at a crouch, Hector spread out & helpless, there came from below sudden piercing squeals of delight and terror, as a pack of hysterical hermaphrodites—later said to have been dope-injected by the Purity Police—charged down upon the guest-strewn field. The screaming grew in crescendo, and when the pitch of ecstasy reached a certain level, the plastic dome which covered all & everyone shattered, shivered, and torrents of rain whipped down upon them mixed with obscene white crumbs.

Chapter 8

——————————▶ Richard Calvin was a man who knew his limitations. It gave him pain that so many others, chief among them Hector Bloom, wouldn't know theirs. If as a teacher he could impart to each student some sense of painful shortcoming, he would consider himself not unsuccessful in his worldly vocation.

Outside of the scholarly world, the impact of Richard Calvin's researches would not be earthshaking, but that fact only canceled the suspense he might have felt and gave him a happy control over what he was doing. He was able to work hard, to work the same hours every day, and thus—as he charted his progress—to project his life in minute detail five years in advance. In exactly sixteen months, his first major book, *Tragedy and the Modern Predicament in Poetry*, would be published. In twenty-three months, he would have tenure. In thirty months, his second child would have to be conceived, and in thirty-nine months, born. In fifty-four months he would take his first sabbatical, which he would spend courtesy of a special grant in Milan, doing research for his third book. Already he was after his wife to write for hotel reservations.

Richard was an Assistant Professor in the Classics Dept, where he taught mainly the Great Works of Western Man in Translation Survey Course for Freshmen. To keep up his morale, he was also allowed to teach courses from time to time in Greek Drama, Stoic Philosophy, and Horace. He worshiped Horace, in moderation. Richard had spotted Hector Bloom in Hector's sophomore year when Hector was in one of Richard's sections of Great Works II, the sophomore survey course. He was attracted by the young man's brightness and energy, and resolved to take him under his wing. He soon confided to his wife that he was worried about Hector: Hector was not only irresponsible, he *insisted* on being irresponsible. He did not simply fall into his mistakes, like other people; he willed them.

It was obvious that Hector would have to undergo a self-awakening which would change him drastically. From time to time, Richard Calvin would drop a hint to this effect, and Hector would pick it up, but, exasperatingly, nothing would happen, or so it seemed. The Friday following the Sunday of the traumatic party at Moses Mandel's estate, however, there arose an occasion which seemed to cry out for Professor Calvin's therapeutic efforts. Hector Bloom had absented himself, as was his occasional wont, from the two previous class meetings that week, thereby depriving himself of material indispensable to the organization of the course. The Friday session started without him, but after fifteen minutes he made an entrance looking somewhat startled, as though he had expected to find himself in the men's washroom. His appearance was disgraceful:

his hair was conspicuously uncombed, and his attire was incorrect. Not bothering to remove his coat, which he had not bothered to button or put his arms through, he wandered vaguely to a seat in the back of the room, fell bodily into it, and sat staring intensely out the window in an attitude of total and absorbing personal depression. Under his arm, Hector clutched a battered paper-covered copy of *Moby Dick*. A red flag before the bull: Richard Calvin was brutally insulted, and, for a moment, speechless with fury. But he struggled to compose himself, and was instantly rewarded by an illumination that would enable him to turn the lesson into a true lesson.

This was his Greek Tragedy course, and he had been lecturing on Sophocles. "But the tragic type is universal," he continued, "because the tragic experience can recur whenever an individual is sufficiently powerful and lunatic to bring it upon himself. For the tragic hero is always deranged. Classic American literature furnishes a perfect example of him in Captain Ahab of *Moby Dick*. Like Oedipus, Ahab is clearly insane. He is a monomaniac, pursuing a single idea past all social or humane considerations. In his fanatic pursuit of the white whale he repeatedly violates the natural order of the universe, as expressed both in his own mortal limitations, and in the limitations of his men and his ship. For this he is punished: first with the loss of a leg—symbolic of man's redeeming sexual connection with woman—then with the loss of human society, and finally with the loss of his life, and, presumably, his immortal soul. That is why the reader feels a certain relief, a certain satisfaction, when the Pequod sinks to the bottom. The natural order of the universe has reasserted itself, the hero who wouldn't adjust has been crushed, and things are as they should be."

Dr Calvin paused, and watched the lesson sink home. Here was his chief reason for liking Hector Bloom: Bloom could always be disturbed. Hector flushed heavily beneath his dark skin, his red eyes glared, and he mumbled, "relief! . . . satisfaction?"

"Do you have a question, Mr Bloom?"

"Uh . . . yeah. Will you describe in a little more detail *how things are?*"

Hector's confusion would best be handled by friendly laughter. "We have only five minutes left this period, Mr Bloom!" The teacher was rewarded by a burst of spontaneous laughter from his class. Hector looked down at his feet, and Richard Calvin was satisfied that his point had been made.

Always a generous winner, Prof Calvin approached the still-brooding Hector after class. "When are you coming to see our baby?" he asked. He invited the young man to dinner that very night.

After practice that afternoon, Hector met Gabriel in their room and told him they would not be able to eat supper together.

"Hey!" said Gabriel. "Take me with you!"

"Why?"

"Because if Calvin's woman is who I think she is, she'll be pretty damn happy to see me. She's just about our age, you know: Calvin grabbed her right out of college."

"So how do you know her?"

"I met her at a fraternity convention in Louisville two years ago. God what a fantastic body! A Southern belle, man, she endureth! We had rented a whole fucking hotel. She was drunk with me one night in my room. But I never took the chance! No guts. You know, I never take advantage of my opportunities. I never even know they *are* opportunities till years and years later!"

"She was wild for you?"

"Wild? Man, she would have done anything, anything! But I wasn't even aware. If only I had known!"

"If only," Hector agreed.

They arrived at the Calvins' fifteen minutes late; everyone else was there already.

"Where WERE you!" shouted Richard Calvin as he opened the door. "Now everything is cold!" He was wearing his happy scolding smile, which quickly faded when he saw Gabriel Reuben.

"We'll have to set another plate," he said. "Sylvie! Sylvie! Do we have enough for seven?"

Richard ran around a little half-cocked over the astounding typical rudeness of Hector Bloom in inviting an extra person for supper. Hector and Gabriel busily shook hands with the assembled guests. There were only three: Paul & Christine Felix, a pair of gentle young folksingers, who scraped by on Paul's earnings from the one course on American Folk Customs the University hired him to teach, and Richard Calvin's number one protégé, a graduate student and lady poetess named Rosetta Stein, whom Hector recognized had been invited especially for *his* delectation. Rosetta was a fluffy, dainty thing, muffled in angora sweater in hopes of making sex out of a trifle plumpness. The Felixes, too, were pets of the Calvins, captured by Richard and too nice to know they were uncomfortable. They were so mild and honorable they scarcely knew they were poor.

Gabriel immediately started talking with Paul Felix about the labor songs of the thirties, and Paul Felix lay back his fragile head and dreamily recalled some hard-lipped lyrics:

> . . . *if you don't let red-baiting*
> *break you up*
> *And if you don't let stoolpigeons*
> *break you up*
> *And if you don't let vigilantes*
> *break you up*
> *And if you don't let race-hatred*
> *break you up*

> *YOU'LL WIN!*

"Yes yes," whispered Gabriel. " 'What I mean is: take it easy, but take it.' "

"But how simple it was in those days!" Hector burst out enviously. *How simple to win a victory you could enjoy!* " 'Just pass out a leaflet and call a meetin!' If you did that today, no one'd come—they'd all be home washing their cars and watching television!"

"That's because they *did win*, more or less," put in Richard Calvin from the kitchen, where he was helping his wife. "They got enough wages to buy TV sets and cars—and then they could afford to sit back and be national guardsmen, race-haters and vigilantes like everyone else."

"Speak for yourself, dad," said Gabriel.

"Oh I dunno," drawled Paul Felix. "It wasn't simple then, and it isn't simple now. . . ."

Loaded with plates, Richard scuttled past them and into the dining room, where they could see him frantically trying to redistribute the already-set table so that it would be divided heptagonally. Suddenly from behind them came a tremendous wail, and Richard darted back through the living room, chortling with glee, and emerged again with a bawling bundled red pucker-faced baby. He held the baby all around so everyone could see it, and said, both to it and to them: ". . . isn't oo snookums! isn't oo snookums! ooooooo isn't oo snookums! ooo ess oo is, ess oo is! oo is snook-snook-snookums! oo is snook-snook-snookums!"

Gabriel said, "I don't care whether it's a boy or a girl, it's a girl."

But Richard didn't hear him. He staggered back, holding the baby at arm's length, as a great wet stain spread down his arm to match the one on his chest. "Sylvie! Sylvie!" he screamed, and his wife came in from the kitchen. Despite the frenzy of his call she moved with unshakable deliberation. Her breasts and hips were ample, her body slow, complete unto itself, her eyes large and furry and childlike and otherworldly as one of Gauguin's South Sea women. Gabriel stared fascinated at the great child-woman she had become. Offhandedly she took the baby from her husband and took it away and changed it and without looking handed it back to him. It was still crying. Richard said, "Sylvie, she's still crying, stop crying sweetie, stop crying, stop crying, that's it stop crying stop crying stop it now daddy says stop it now, Sylvie do you hear me she's still crying what's wrong, stop crying sweetie, daddy says stop it stop it now stop crying stop . . ."

Sylvia nodded to Gabriel. "Hii," she said, unsurprised, and put a motherly kiss on Hector's forehead, in keeping with the Official Calvin Attitude on Young Hector Bloom. Actually she was not far from his own age but seemed intangibly older. Richard had told Hector that after years of patient research, he had finally spotted Sylvie while visiting Kentucky for a poetry conference. He had decided at once to sweep her off her feet. To Hector Sylvie seemed self-enclosed. She was the kind of woman who made you want to bang hell out of her: she had it coming. Though Sylvie was not really bitchy—did she care enough to bitch? One just had to get to know her, Richard kept saying, yet somehow one never could—only he, Richard . . . Richard was the only one who would not push her. He loved her for herself alone. That was why she let him, of all men, of so many men, choose her. All the others had wanted something—to crack her, beat her, solve her secret. For Richard, marriage and household were adornment in plenty. He came to her, he confessed, fully as virgin as she to him.

Richard & Sylvie retired to the kitchen now where Hector could hear him whispering his last-minute instructions. The brief recognition he had gotten from Sylvie had momentarily unhinged Gabriel, who paced oblivious up and down the room, like a disturbed giraffe. After a while the contents of the room itself began to register on him, and he turned to Hector grinning. The living room was a perfection of itself: with its symmetric corner couches split around an end table, varnished coffee table, bulbous ceramic lamp and aluminum pole lamp, wall-to-wall beige matting and bookcases of neat-dusted jacketless blue-backed hard-cover books. Overhead on the ceiling fixture: a shiny brass deflector. On the wall: a framed Picasso print, a Modigliani and a small ceramic. On all the little lamp tables: manufactured wooden African heads, white Danish vases, Israeli ashtrays.

The cherrywood dining table was set with bamboo place mats. Sylvie & Richard reentered with white glass bowls to match their white curved pottery plates. Their guests dined on a magnificent meal of chicken *rambasconi* with garlic bread on the side. All through the *rambasconi* Richard talked about the food, interrogating his guests about just how good it was ("Honestly now!"), recalling & analyzing times when the same dish was made just a little better, recounting comic incidents revolving around Sylvie's learning to cook when she first married him, and constantly filling plates with fresh moderate helpings.

After the main course, Richard produced a tureen crammed full of substance, which he announced as "a special salad dressing, invented in honor of the occasion."

"My God!" said Christine Felix, trying her salad and blushing. "What did you put in it?"

"Oh mostly mayonnaise and ketchup, plus a few secret ingredients which must remain nameless."

While the salad was being disposed of, Richard struck up a conversation with Hector concerning Moses Mandel's party.

"Wasn't that a nice party?" he said.

"Nice?"

"I mean the house and the food and everything. Everything was so pretty."

"I was scared."

"Oh well, perhaps the fun got a little bit out of hand at the end there. But I'm no prude. It's healthy for people to cut loose once in a while; I don't believe in constant seriousness. And I was glad to see some of the people there. Of course the old man is a clown, but I enjoyed talking with the Solomons; I like them, though I think Morton has not yet drawn the logical conclusion from his political premises. But he will. And don't you like Olive? I find I like her better as time goes by. Don't you think she's improved, Sylvie? She's much better now. It's nice to see how Olive's settled down."

Gabriel choked on his salad and losing his balance fell

purple-faced into Rosetta Stein's consternated lap. As Richard got up and pounded the poor boy's back, Hector noticed a proprietary gleam in his eye.

"Give him some water!" Richard cried. Rosetta Stein rushed off to the bathroom and returned with a glass of water fifteen minutes later.

"By the way, Hector," Richard said, "have you given serious thought to turning pro?"

"Huh?"

"I mean next year. I'm sure you've had feelers."

"Hhmmn!" Hector said.

"You know Sylvie and I were talking it over, and I absolutely agree with her: you ought to do it."

"I thought you wanted to make me a professor of classics?"

"That's just it. Believe me, Hector, it will be at least five years before you'll make a decent salary out of teaching. You could starve. What you ought to do is play professional basketball while going to graduate school out of season. You'll have unbelievable security!"

"But when will I live?" Hector inquired.

Richard looked sadly and fondly upon him. " 'When I was a child, I spake as a child: but when I became a man, I put away childish things,' " he quoted.

"I was only joking," Hector said.

Richard smiled affectionately and squeezed Hector's arm.

"Sylvie, don't you think Hector is getting more mature?"

Dinner was over, and Hector helped Sylvie & Richard carry the dishes into the kitchen. Richard was in an expansive mood. He was talking about Gabriel, and obviously trying to integrate the young man into his hospitality. "I didn't know you knew Gabriel," he said to his wife. "You must be good to him. I sense he needs someone to talk to."

In the living room again, Richard leaned back and told them: "Now that we're getting to be friends, I'll tell you something. This is my night of fun. Quiet now, Sylvie, I'm going to tell them. You see, I work six days a week on my book at the same hours each night, and confidentially I'm getting to hate it. Now this is the seventh night and I am bound to *have fun!* And I want *everyone* to have fun! EVERYONE HAS TO BE JOLLY!"

There was something of a pall. But Richard demanded, "Okay?" and in return there were a few sounds of "uh . . . okay."

"Hell no," said Hector. "I never had a good time in my life!"

"I know what!" said Gabriel, clapping his hands together. "Let's turn off the lights and play spin-the-bottle!"

"No!" Richard leapt to his feet. "I have a much jollier idea! We'll all make our own sundaes for dessert. What's a meal without a good dessert? We'll jump in the car and we'll rush down to the supermarket and buy the yummiest sqooshiest yummiest stuff in the world!

"Isn't that WONDERFUL!"

And in a twinkling he had them hustled out of the house and packed snug into his car heading for the shopping center. Gabriel was delirious because it turned out he had Sylvie on his lap, but the less fortunate Paul Felix had his hands full extracting Rosetta Stein's elbow from his Adam's apple. Soon Richard had them running up and down the aisles like escapees from the lunatic orphans' home, comparing prices of canned & boxed nuts, maraschino cherries & preserves, various kinds & flavors of ice cream, whipping cream & poof-top-box whipped cream.

In order to survive Hector trotted mechanically up the aisles and around the shelves, keeping always a wall or two of shelves between himself and the shouting voices, taking care to steer himself clear of the pink cold patches near the meat bins or the slippery spot on the floor by the instant-ice machine. He could hear Gabriel shouting "Yes, man, yes! Buy buy buy!" Women fled from the area, rushing their shopping carts and babies ahead of them.

"We're having fun," Richard explained to the cashier. "Who but us could have so much fun!" he cried to his cohorts.

"Holy bananas!" shouted Gabriel.

Richard finally figured the cheapest possible purchase, and extracted 45¢ per head for ½ gallon mixed chocolate & French vanilla ice cream, one 5-ounce sack shelled pecans, 1 carton heavy cream (for whipping), 4 bananas, a small bottle cherries, and some powder to mix with milk to make chocolate sauce. Richard said they could use his milk for the chocolate sauce. Preserves, coconut, almonds, tutti-frutti and whipped-cream bombs were ruled out on account of extravagance.

They whipped on home now jollier than ever, Paul Felix striking up a three-jolly-coachmen song until he got poked in the diaphragm on a tight corner.

Back to the house where they waited in jolly suspense while what Richard named the Preparing Committee made their sundaes. From the kitchen they could hear Rosetta Stein moaning in famished ecstasy: "Oh my diet . . . my diet. . . ." And here at last she stepped in bearing them and blushing and were they ever ooshy-gooshy delicious!

"How about some booze?" asked Hector.

"That would be even jollier, but it's so expensive. Who but us could have such deliciousness all by ourselves for so little? I bet this would cost ninety-five cents at O'Connor's!"

"More," said Rosetta. "A dollar fifty at least."

"Fifteen dollars and a hand job for O'Connor," opined Gabriel.

"Yum yum yum," said Richard.

"Besides," Sylvie said, "Heck-tuh's in training!"

"That's right!" Richard said. *And we must take such good care of good good Hector!*

By nine-thirty everyone had managed to find a reason to leave. Richard didn't notice. "It's so wonderful," he beamed, with an arm around Hector and an arm around Gabriel, "when we can have a fine time and still go to bed on schedule, ready to get up and go in the morning!"

"You know what I would like to do?" said Gabriel as they drove back to the gym. "I'd like to crawl on my hands & knees through a field of those breasts!"

"Oh motha!" moaned Hector.

"Let me have the car!" Gabriel said. "I'll drop you off."

"Okay." Hector was tired. As he stumbled out of the car he was hit from above by a new wave of exhaustion and felt his legs crumple as he walked. A light sleet had begun to fall and he felt it sliver like daggers on the back of his neck and rush on down his spine. He was cold, he wanted warmth. For the first Friday night in five years he would be in bed by eleven o'clock. *All I want is a person, a person, a real person. . . .* But the words grew more & more meaningless with his numbness, and by the time he stumbled into bed he wanted no one at all, just himself and warmth and sleep.

Chapter 9

━━━━━━━━━━━━━━▶ Hector had crawled deep
inside the cave, far from the small opening where light
came. Struggling to look around, he saw vague shadows
passing dimly on the far far wall. He yearned to hold them,
look at them, talk to them. Were they people?

Chapter 10

━━━━━━━━━━▶ Gabriel was going to take a chance. He drove straight back to the Calvins'.

Gabriel knocked, and stood waiting a full minute while scurrying went on inside, as though he had surprised a pair of wee animals in their den. His night of fun, thought Gabriel. Sylvie Calvin opened the door clutching her bathrobe.

"What do you want?" she said. "Cain't you come back tomorrow? We're asleep."

"I must talk to you," Gabriel said. "Alone. Put on some clothes and come out with me."

"Gay-brell, don't be silly. This is no time for conversation. Go 'way and come back tomorrow. You hear? You can talk all you like then."

"Sylvie!" cried Richard from within. "Who is it? What's the matter?" He, too, came to the door in his bathrobe.

"May I come in?" Gabriel asked.

"Well, I suppose so. But we're asleep."

They went into the living room. Neither man sat, and Sylvie Calvin headed straight for the bedroom.

"Sylvie, come back!" cried Gabriel. Mustering up his old training, he came onto Richard all square & sincere.

"You know, Dr Calvin, your wife is an old friend of mine. I came back because I've got to talk to her about something. It's a matter of grave personal importance. Is it all right with you if she comes for a drive with me?"

"What do you say, honey?" said Richard Calvin to Sylvie Calvin.

"I declare I cain't see why it cain't wait till morning."

Her reply irritated Richard, for he was determined to cure her of what he thought her shyness: to open her up so that she might radiate to others the warmth & well-being of their marriage.

"But we have things to do tomorrow," he reminded her. "Perhaps you really ought to throw on some clothes and go for a little walk with Gabriel. One really can't say no when one is needed."

Without a word, Sylvie turned and went to get dressed. Richard smiled benevolently. "If there's anything I can do. . . ."

"No, I think not. All I need is the right person to talk to."

"Sylvie is a wonderfully sensitive person, isn't she? I'm glad you've seen that—not everyone does."

Sylvie came out wearing a cotton shift and a sullen expression. She wore no stockings, Gabriel saw, and likely no underclothing. She pouted, shifted her hips: the sharecropper's daughter in a potato sack. Gabriel was aroused right then & there. He quickly turned his back and walked toward the door.

"Don't forget, honey!" warned Richard in parting. "You've got to get up when I do tomorrow morning to do the laundry. I thought if we both finished early we'd take a drive to that pretty state forest!"

Sylvia leaned against the car window and sulked. Gabriel drove very rapidly down the highway feeling every minute more & more desperate. He could not think of a single word to say to this woman, nor imagine why he had ever thought she might like him. She was bored with him because he didn't know what to say and had no guts to begin. It was impossible to go back, and yet there was nowhere to go on to. To forestall a showdown, Gabriel headed up the drive of Lucky Larry Lacy's all-night drive-in movie-drome, which had just that week installed a gigantic Dewdrop Saf-T-Dome. A blinking, whirling electric sign announced the guarantee:

WE PROTECT OUR PATRONS

SAFE AND SOUND

FROM

GERMS

GAS

FALLOUT

OR MONEY BACK

They sat and watched the last reel of an inept-father situation comedy. Father has a wild plan for making money lots of money, which it seems would utterly wreck the family and leave affairs as tangled as the fishing tackle which falls on him and ties him up when he tries to get into a closet. Fortunately, however, his daughters are cool like Mommy, and they attend to the happy resolution, which involves old vest-tightened father going back to the office he never really hated after all and daughters each evaporating with the firm-jawed pencil-eyed man of her choice while Mom is the one who gets the money and rolls on into the sunset invincible.

Oh what an Ass is father! A nice guy okay, but you gotta feel sorry for him. So pathetic, the way he tries to get outa it & don't know what to do! Got troubles, better ask Mom. . . .

"All right now, what do you want?" Sylvia said. Gabriel had dreaded this for so long he was resigned and had no answer ready.

"Sylvie, I want to talk with you," he stalled. A cartoon began, with chase music. A great, nasty tomcat was chasing a pair of genius mice.

"Well talk," she said.

"Well look," he said. He put his arm around her shoulders but she did not move any part of her body in the slightest, nor look at him.

"Sylvie look," he said, not knowing exactly what he would say next. "I can't understand what you're doing with yourself. [pause: no answer] I mean like . . . like you're one of the most . . . like you're a real *woman!*"

"Am I? A real one?"

"Not when you answer like that!"

"But you're the one who wants to talk, honey chile. I want to sleep."

"You'll have years to sleep! All your life! So listen to me. I dig you better than you think. You'd take a fearful chance responding to me, a fearful chance. But you haven't got any choice, baby, you've got to, I mean no matter what apple carts get upset."

"I swear I don't know what you're talking about. Your eyes are rolling all around your head."

"Sweetheart, we're in the same bag. I want you. You need a man and I want you."

At this he kissed her, and would not let himself be surprised when she didn't resist him. He took her stillness as a sign of bashfulness, so that when he put her hand on his groin and she left it there, it meant sweet acquiescence, which was all Gabriel had ever known for a go-ahead sign. So he ran straight on through his intercourse, by the numbers, not noticing that his partner was giving in through indifference and malice and maybe spite at her husband for putting her there in the first place. He would not let himself notice, got it all done too fast to notice, slinging his baggage in the receptacle right away, no sooner than the booming title music came from the screen to signify the beginning of *I Was a Teenage Pederast*, his anxious lightning providing for Sylvie a moment of spectatorly irony, coming as it did exactly as quick as Richard's, the only difference being that with Gabriel there was steadfastly no sense of shortcoming or regret. Yet.

After that there was no reason for words, but Gabriel figured that by the law of completed aggression he had triumphed, and unfortunately couldn't resist the desire to run through a few more emotions.

Driving back on the deserted highway, he asked her, "Let's make it again, baby, shall we? You're not gonna forget me, like I mean never!"

"No."

"Like No, you won't forget me?"

"No, like No, we won't be making it."

"Why," said Gabriel, "you little bitch."

"Look," he said. "You know something? I'm not interested in you really, except as a cunt. That's all you are to me, a velvet-lined vulva. Like personally you zero, baby, you don't score, nothing. You think I'm going to ride in and break you out of your sack, like they say in the fairy books, but you're wrong, like baby you just don't know how wrong you are. Truth I'm just going to *have* you, because baby you feel good!"

He pulled off the road and stopped the car and sat glaring at her, she sitting calm with her knees drawn up looking straight ahead at the unmoving blackness in front of them. Gabriel held himself together inside like a fist and softly began telling her that he needed her, that they were great together, that he loved her, that he loved the feel of her, that he wanted to take her far away and keep her by him forever. Easing a little, he told her that she was cold, that she was making him miserable. There was a choke in his voice at this point, but still she did not reply.

He described her body for her: the loveliness of her breasts like hard pillows, the curve of her belly, her strong hips, and finally as he talked he slid his hand way up inside her dress again and began softly to caress her belly.

She sighed.

"Can we go home now?" she said. "I'm tired."

He slugged her. It was only proper. But instead of staying slugged, she slugged him right back. He grabbed her arms, and exerting all his strength wrestled her to a standstill and lying hard upon her tried to force her, but she suddenly went limp as a dishrag, boneless, with knowing contempt in her eyes and on her lips. At the sudden brute ugliness of her giving-in the passion of Gabriel straightaway dried up and withered on the vine. His penis folded like an accordion and his testicles retracted into their cavities like the two front legs of an old, scared turtle. For a moment they lay face to face, sweating in each other's armpits. He trembling, she with an enigmatic smile.

The only thing left for him was to drive her home. The air was grey and tingling, a cube of slate waiting to be smashed by the yellow sledgehammer dawn. He shoved her violently out of the car, and as she walked deliberately up the flagstone path not looking back ever, he shouted coolly into the tidy suburban waking-up, loud enough so her neighbors might hear and shiver in their sheets: "You ice-cold fucking bitch. Sylvia Calvin: you freezing-cold sexless sterile cocksnatching virgin!"

Then he turned around and, drove into the fire of the new-risen sun, going suddenly mad as a flock of insane dawn-chirping birds rose all around him enveloping the car, he aching with fatigue and insanity, and thinking again and again as he sank into depression how great she was how great she was how great how *great* she was.

Inside the house Richard Calvin stirred at Sylvie's slow precise footsteps and stumbled out of bed to release the chain. "Where WERE you?" he cried.

"What did he say? What did he want to talk about?"

"Later," said his wife.

And so they went to bed, he lying awake and musing beside her relaxed heavily sleeping form, daring occasionally to run an unobtrusive hand over the line of her hips. He was enthralled by her mystery. Here, he thought triumphantly, is a *real* woman!

As for Gabriel, he fell upon his bed and wept.

"I can't feel anything," he sobbed. "I'm a cartoon!"

Chapter 11

━━━━━━━━━▶ The trainer shaved all the hair off his upper leg, and wound a thick bandage round his thigh. Hector wouldn't let him tape his ankles.

He put his shoes on carefully. Mustn't bunch the socks or he'd get blisters.

Laced up the high tops. The socks were clean and everything felt snug. His elastic jockstrap held him at the waist and kept his balls on. The practice uniform had been washed, too, and smelt like a laundry. The sweatsuit was warm and covered up his limbs.

None of the others was there, and as he bounced up the iron steps from the lockerroom to the gym floor, the separate clanks echoed lonely metal sounds. He could feel his toes pressing him upward and the arch of his foot.

He scooped up a ball and stood there stretching it over his head, whirling it in one hand then another with his arms stiff as semaphores. Leaning over backwards to wake up his back muscles, then bouncing the ball very low and fast off the floor in little figure eights around his feet.

He liked to take some shots all alone. He had learned to shoot alone on the darkening California concrete long after the others had gone home to supper, on into the dark, when his red cat's eyes needed no help but the moon's. Silver moonshine—the ghostly silver cords flipping as an invisible ghost ball passed through.

He wasn't really warm yet—he was lazy, basically lazy, and needed the press of others to warm him. It was mostly for his fingers that he came up early by himself—his fingers had a special something with the ball and they had to meet each other privately. They had to say hello and feel each other out. When Hector was in a hurry, he knew he was chancing it might be no go.

He took a couple of stretchy hook shots, without aiming —one with the right, one with the left hand. The cuffs of the sweatsuit felt tight and sweet on his wrists. But the bandage threw him off balance. *Damn*: he resented it like a defense that hung on his back all night. *A big train pulls so many passengers. . . .*

"Chug chug chug chug chug chug chug chug chug chug," he said to himself, as he tried a series of short jump-shots. He let the ball bounce away, and cupping his hands made a locomotive whistle, beautifully shrill & enormous in the high-beamed field house.

He stood right under the backboard and tossed up hundreds of lay-ups on both sides of the basket and from the front, hardly ever bored. It was a constant wonderment to him how infinite were the ways and angles of bouncing the ball off the backboard and into the basket. And his fingers were flexing. Occasionally he would spin the ball like a globe on one fingertip, then let it roll down the arm and across his back and out into his other hand. He jumped easily off his feet and stuffed the ball down through the basket, then went back again to lay-ups. Frequently he missed, to his fascination. After about two hundred lay-ups he began bouncing the ball high off the backboard and tapping it back into the basket. There was no noise: he cupped his hand and cushioned each ball on his fingertips as he tapped it through. Everything depended on the feel in his fingertips and the control when his wrist straightened. And his timing: to get the ball at exactly the right time & place.

He could see right through the glass backboard and into the vacant stands behind. It looked almost as though the ball were stopped by an invisible hand that took his pass and made the score. But Hector did not indulge that kind of illusion; he had made the play so many times the board was real to him whether he saw it or not, real as the ball which he dribbled and never looked at while dribbling so as to be constantly ready for the shift or the shot or the pass. He saw through the board to the stands and the shadows, but he knew the board was there, and he kept right on working at it and getting better and enjoying getting better.

While he was working on his tips his teammates began to drift in and collect at the basket at the opposite end of the floor. It was their custom to stay clear of Hector till he was ready.

Suddenly Hector knew that Goose Jefferson was at the bottom of the stairway.

He stood waiting with his back to the stairwell for two seconds, then threw the ball over his head so that it took one long bounce into the corner of the gym and would have fallen straight down the stairs had not Goose Jefferson emerged at just that instant, caught the ball without surprise, and dribbled straight over to lay it in the basket.

Goose and Hector passed the ball back and forth and took lazy shots at the basket. Goose had the way of the great Negro ballplayers of going up in the air and shooting only after he had stayed in the air a few seconds longer than anyone's nerves would have figured him to. It went like this: Goose in the air and the defensive man right with him, then the defensive man down and Goose still there, finally shooting. He seemed to *hang*, perhaps the result of a couple of centuries of moving with a rope tugging at his neck.

Hector stayed up too, in his own way. His was more a bounce than a glide; instead of hanging he seemed simply to keep going up. Often he could grab a rebound off the defensive boards, pivot on his way down, dribble up court while the others were still turning around, and catch maybe only one or two men back on defense. They would cluster near the basket and when he got to the foul line Hector would take off, sailing right up over their heads, either passing off at the last moment to a teammate left unguarded in his wake, or else shifting the ball from one hand to the other and cramming it down through the hoop.

There were six boys at the far basket now and six more at one off to the side. They were playing three on three; Hector and Goose stopped to watch them. The boys played basketball white-boss style. There are only two styles of basketball in America, and of the two the white-boss grimly prevails over the Negro. The loose lost Negro style, with its reckless beauty, is the more joyful to watch or play, if you can, but it is the white-boss style that wins. Even the Negroes must play white-boss basketball to win, though fortunately the best ones can't, and end up with both, the Negro coming out despite themselves right on top of the other style. And it is these boss Negro players who are the best in the world, the artists of basketball, the ones every pro team needs two or three or six of if it is to stay beautiful and win.

The boys were *hustling* for all they were worth: that's the first essential of white-boss basketball. He who wants to relax and enjoy it is gonna be left behind, or knocked over and his ball ripped away from him. For white bosses play very rough. Unlike Negroes, they will not back off and let a man keep the rebound he has jumped for: they'll tackle him, lean on his back slap at his hands tie up his arms, hoping to wrestle away his prize. And even before the rebound, the grim jostling and bumping for position. A good white-boss basketball player is a good football player— deadly, brutal and never satisfied. What keeps him going is the thought that he and no one else must always win, every instant. Let him win twenty games and he will sulk and cry and kick down the referees' lockerroom door because he did not win the twenty-first. So by definition there can be no enjoyment. Can't you hear those bloodcurdling screams from the stands where thousands are tied in by their legs? They scream not for pleasure but revenge. Revenge for a crime that is committed fast as it can be wiped away. Because for every winner there is a loser, and then it is the winner who must pay, sooner or later, and on & on & on, right up to heaven *vs.* hell.

O sweet godgod, thought Hector, *this is my heaven right here!* He swished a blind hook shot from the middle of the floor, and for a moment felt better. *No matter how I feel!*

heaven, i'm in heaven, & my heart beats so that i can hardly think. . . .

and Olive and raving Moby Dick plunging fathoms where

*my father lies in shit-sweet ice cream, the furnace drying up
my brain cells into sand grains up which crawls and trickles
down the satellite bleeding into beaches, for Gabriel, for
the moon, for the American Revolution in amazing new
endless garden party, food food food stuffed into nostrils
and the whole miserable busy worldmeal I can hardly drink
food drink!*

Kiss me, Jesus, by chance I'm still alive!

At this point Fighting Coach Jack Bullion entered the
gymnasium. His blood had not the slightest drop of black.
His hearth gods were Discipline and Teamwork. His line
of scripture was, "If you don't hear from me, you're doing
fine; 'cause if you screw up, you'll hear plenty!" He liked
to sneak up behind his players and shout, "Wake up! What
the hell you think you're doing!" Even the most competent
ballplayers glanced at the bench each time they made a mistake, to see if a substitute were getting up. Before Hector
came, the players used to pass the ball through carefully
rehearsed patterns for five minutes, then either take the shot
they had in the first place or lose possession. Hector Bloom
was the only player in Coach Bullion's career who remained
absolutely unaffected by his coaching; for—*much as I like
to think differently*—his ups and downs depended entirely
on what went on inside him.

The boys at the other end played twice as hard and twice
as bad when Coach Bullion came on the scene. They would
play on ferocious, all their lives, hustling on & on, right up to
heaven *vs.* hell, because even as babies they had it printed in
their little minds that someone is guilty, someone must pay,
someone must lose, someone must take the blame. And Oh
God, Oh God, each one prayed inside himself, if I can try
just a little harder let it not be me!

Coach Bullion walked in with his legs spread and stood

planted. He wore basketball shoes and a big baggy pair of sweatpants, a T-shirt with "COACH" on it and a silver whistle hanging down on his expansive chest and paunch. His head was getting bald and covered by a short-peaked baseball cap, but around his neck and where the sleeves ended on his arms the black and white tufted hair crept out and rioted.

He called the team around him and explained how lousy they looked and how badly they were going to get beaten the next night.

Then began the calisthenics. They circled the empty gym doing the good old American duck walk, the exercise of grasshoppers that bulges the thighs and ruins the knees for life. Then the sit-ups and the stretching, with a partner clamping the feet while each in turn stretched and turned and stretched and turned in panicked time to numbers that were always just a little too fast. Then flat on your bellies, hold your ankles in your hands and rock to & fro on your tummies. Thirty push-ups, up down up downup, get that ass in! Over on your backs, legs straight, feet three inches off the floor. Hold it . . . hold it . . . now keep on holding it and clap your stomachs. Feels nice, heh heh, doesn't it? Okay everyone running in place, faster, knees up to chest, faster faster! NOW FALL FLAT! TEN PUSH-UPS! UP AGAIN & RUNNING! FASTER!

After half an hour they were permitted to sprawl flat and rest thirty seconds, then up and twenty laps at good speed around the gym. They were sweaty and beaten and when Luther Nixon emptied his big canvas sack and passed out the basketballs they were grateful as orphans climbing up on Santa Claus. The first drill involved sets of three men each and was designed to practice ball-handling and fast-breaking. Each man ran full speed straight down the floor, one in the middle and one on either side, passing the ball to the center and out, to the center and out with no dribbling, till they got to the end and one man took a final pass and laid it in. The whole thing took three seconds and five passes, and by the time one trio got past center court another would begin from the end line. After each man went through five runs at each position, Coach Bullion decided on a two-man defense, Hector Bloom and Goose Jefferson, as a punishment for their not hustling. Hector and Goose stood one on each side as the trios came down on them and tried to break up the play before a shot could be gotten off, or, failing that, to force a bad shot and grab off the rebound. They didn't mind, really, and began unstringing the boys with Indian whoops, small ones, whoopwhoopwhoop, and broke up eight plays in a row. But still they came, one trio after another bearing down with them having to pick themselves up and momentumless defend the same position time after time: it got wearing and they began to sag, save their breath, play it safe and let the middle man come just a little closer inside the foul line where he could score and did. And at each score Coach Bullion would stop everything and send Hector and Goose Jefferson around the gym in a duck walk. Whupwhupwhup, mimicked the delighted unpunished boss boys, who knew nothing of Indians. Eventually Hector said No, and there was a silence, and Coach Bullion said What did you say? . . . and Hector Boom said I prefer not to, and there was a long silent pause and Hector Bloom turned and walked into the corner of the gym and kicked something inanimate while Coach Bullion switched to another drill.

Plays had to be practiced, whether or not they would actually be used in a game, to protect the team from fear of improvisation. So they split into three teams of five and dry-ran their plays for half an hour with no shooting allowed until after five passes, while a manager counted and Coach Bullion blew on his silver whistle and stopped everyone so he could shout at a wrongdoer.

Still not ready for a scrimmage: the first team played defense in a half-court game while the second and third teams tried to run off the plays they'd been practicing. Again, the five-pass rule, which usually gave the regulars time to disarm the play before it started, and again more shouting and blaming. At first some of the plays worked, but as more corrections were added and more movements inhibited, things went worse and worse, until finally a fifteen-minute stretch went by without a basket. The second and third teams duckwalked ten times around the gym and sprinted two lengths of the floor backwards while the first team took their first free shots since practice officially began.

At last the scrimmage, with the second team all ashamed and fighting. Coach Bullion played referee and smiled benevolently and refrained from blowing his whistle as the underdogs carved their revenge with elbows and fingernails, proving in capsule both the benefits of insult as education and the rightness of the educator's prediction as to how basically inept his best team would look on the following night.

"You stink!" he shouted at them. "You couldn't beat the House of David Ladies' Auxiliary!"

But they went right on stinking, because they were tired, and because most of them didn't care most of the time. They were sliding down a long season, and the bottom was not yet in sight. All of them carried tape or elastic on some part of their bodies, and four of the five favored an arm or a leg or both. Coach Bullion tried to fire them up by injecting third-string substitutes, but the eager sophomores just got in the way and things went worse than ever. The scrimmage ran on for an hour of plodding up and down the floor, shouting, cursing, giving and taking blows, two fistfights and one disabling injury. By this time there was not a single man on the floor who had any love left in him for his body or what it was doing. As for Hector Bloom, he had been disconnected from the moment he preferred not to.

At six o'clock, three hours after practice had begun, Coach Bullion strode off the court shaking his head in disgust. But before the players could drag themselves into the showers, one hundred freethrows had to be shot by each and every one and the number made recorded by a manager. Luther Nixon in person counted for Hector and passed back the ball, entering his score in an official book that contained the memory of every freethrow Hector had shot since his freshman year. Hector made 71 out of 100 freethrows, whatever that means, before he stumbled off to rejoin himself.

From the beginning the monkeys were howling, 15,000 brass-buttoned monkeys, plus friends, in a far faraway place: "Hector Bloom-Bloom-Bloomble—To Heck with Hector!" Looking for Olive, searching her eyes among 29,998 others searching his. It was not too far to come, *if she really*. . . .

The monkeys were dressed in sweaters and tweed jackets and special haircuts all their each and every own.

Abruptly the warm-up was over. The whole thing had just started, and yet the others were sweating and vibrating and clenching their fists ready to go. Butch Buckholder went around slapping each one on the pants hard: "Come on, guys, let's go!"

Go home?

Home was Yucca Valley, where Irving Bloom had driven during the war to find work in an aircraft plant, and there met his bride, a retired lady welder from the backwoods of Tennessee. *Green Yucca Valley, garden spot of mid-California, where my mother bowls and my father leaves every morning for the city to do whatever it is he does.* Hector couldn't remember forgetting what his father did.

"Bloom! Snap out of it!" Coach Bullion gripped at his arm like a handcuff and tugged at his soul in the rafters.

The State five bounded out on the floor like horses at the starting gate, flexing their pectorals. Bronco Gibbon of State appeared in front of him and mangled his right hand. Hector stood staring at the back of Gibbon's head as the ball was thrown in the air and the game began.

The others had the ball . . . so the thing to do was to run back to the other end of the floor, which was accomplished by throwing the weight forward on alternate legs. Then he faced himself around and waited. State went into their tedious bob-and-weave, playing to bore the defense into letting them through. So Hector went sidestepping following his man as one Stater dribbled & handed off to another Stater who dribbled & handed off to another Stater who . . . Gibbon lowered a shoulder and dribbled straight in. Bouncing Hector for a five-yard loss, he went leisurely into his quaint version of the jump shot, which he loosed from around his navel.

Cowbells, foghorn, & a number of carolers to the tune of "Davy Crockett":

Hec-tor, Hec-tor Bloomberg
King of the La-zy Ass.

Sure, ass anyone. Ass Olive. Olive's ass, so high &
tight. . . .

He was being hemmed into his corner. Bronco from behind bumped with granite stomach; in front backed up the cubical McCoy. When they couldn't get the ball to Hector, a teammate shot from the far corner, and when Hector tried to follow for the rebound, McCoy trailed him and held onto his pants.

"Fuckin' pretty-boy," commented Bronco. He took a short pass and barreled in again. From the floor Hector heard a whistle and saw the little man in the striped shirt go into his crowd-wooing acrobatic routine. The foul was on Hector, and Bronco stepped to the line for two free throws.

The God of Israel is a just God: he'll miss.

Bronco poised still as a stuffed boar amid the tumult, then calmly grimly plumped the ball up. Real sergeant material —made both shots.

But why?

Four minutes went by before Hector got the ball again, and he was vaguely angry. He grabbed a loose ball in the corner and dribbled craftily out and toward the middle. His theory was that one spectacular shot might yet break their backs. Breaking back, stopping, then going full speed he lost Bronco and cut in straight for the basket. The defense rushed to fence him out and he swerved and loosed a long hook shot from the top of the key. It missed everything —rim, backboard, everything.

Hector was curious. *Now how did that happen?*

Perhaps this was all very funny?

But when time-out was called and the team gathered round him and hissed and shook his elbow and while Coach Bullion's pig-fat eyes were shouting up in his face, Hector felt his stomach clamp tight as an oyster. He was far away, seeing himself from the rafters, and his stomach was sending him a message of nausea. *Oh this would all be comic,* said the soul in the rafters; *but it's me, really me,* pulsed the stomach frantically. *Come quickly please please please! No,* said Hector, *I can't accept it.*

This was how he looked to others: the clown, the chief clown. *Olive's wild lovely laugh that I can never quite belong to. . . .*

Sapped with self-hate, saw himself play out half mechanically. Closed out noise, stands, spirit; took part in back-and-forth running, holding up of hands, moving-shifting. Bumped for rebounds. Took safe play, scored two baskets when properly set up and screened. Permitted one thought —that soon it would all be over. Whatever came next could not be so endless as this.

Upset of the Year, Unsung Hero, Overrated Star . . . the typewriters clacked left & right & in a few years it was the half. On the scoreboard, Random State: 49–34. It was customary for players to go down a ramp to sullen crowded visitors' dressing room. *4934: by that time we'll all be dead but this game will still be going on & on . . . on the moon, on Mars. . . .*

Fighting Coach was angry, swelled up all red & cute. Reviled whole team so nice and added special personal nastiness for Mr Guess-who, said to be loafing etc. Threatened. Brought out colored chalk and screeched demented across blackboard unveiling Master Plan for recoupment. Small red manager approached, tried to cram chocolate bar into Hector's yaw. Luther Nixon busy-busy feeding pure oxygen through hoses to tired warriors but not Hector.

Hector took a lemon to suck and sat off behind the lockers in his frozen sweat. He had a vivid picture of hairy arms

& legs and among them himself. He was humiliated, only he didn't care: if it were someone else he would have felt sorry, but since it was only himself it was all right, no need.

Yet, slowly, as he sat, a rage built. His old rage, that had carried him so far. It was a rage at the whole world sitting, the world of spectators, at everything not himself for putting him in the middle and mocking him. And at himself, too, because, beyond the weariness which he could not penetrate, he *did* care, he did he did he did. He had spent too long a life shooting balls into baskets. And so he found himself committed to the final degradation: though he no longer had use for self-respect he was forced to respect the only kind of self he knew, the self he had been given. Or else his only self must die. *Because that was me out there, really me. Like it or not I will have this game to remember of myself.*

Therefore he clenched his fists and fought with all his might against his sickness of himself and his symbols and his deadly soul-fatigue, went back to the game and put his hands in the air and shot as best he could: so that when his team lost, he would not lose. *Not everything, not yet.*

And the funny thing was that later he remembered nothing, absolutely nothing.

Chapter 12

⸻⸻⸻⸻⟶ Gabriel Reuben was waiting
for Hector in the dressing room, his great lustrous eyes filled
with despair. The big bells were beginning to ring out of
tune for Gabriel. He had slipped into one of his colossal
downslides again, and was falling deeper and faster every
second, destined to fall so deep that he would be unable at
last to pull out of it. He had Hector's car waiting and they
fled together to New York for refuge & remorse, not knowing whether they would ever come back. (Three days later
at five o'clock in the morning, Hector drove up the Evacuation Route alone.)

Conrad Hurvey and his leering bald head were established
in new quarters. He opened the door wearing a China-blue
silver-scrolled Oriental robe, with a mad glint in his eye and
his ruby lips smiling like evil cherries. He spoke not a word
but "Baby!" and folded them in.

That first night they walked in on a quiet celebration which marked the end of Conrad Hurvey's winter Zen *sesshin*, or ten-day meditation period, during which he had practiced the customary Zen disciplines. The Valentine brothers were there, but oddly unobtrusive, responding only with dim bye-bye waves, as if they were about to fade into the furniture. The furniture itself was dense, clinging, fastidiously exotic. The apartment was low-ceilinged and many-chambered, shut off from the street by elaborate folding shutters and clouded with a dull rank haze of incense.

There was jazz trickling from somewhere out of sight, cool mouths sucking the marrow from their bones. The beat was slow, feathery, with a light jump of nerves every now & then. From opposite corners of the room crept two horns, one flowing brass and the other thick, purring and then coughing, like a cougar in the night jungle. The two horns intertwined, slipped past each other, ran up and down together striking jolts of soft electricity each time they crossed. There was no acceleration: it was a dance of love between two beautiful and dangerous beasts, who could prowl and prowl and rub infinite shocks of thrill as the current jumped between them, but never stop, and never come to any climax or ending.

Hector was a cat of his own, and jumped his own way. Perhaps his back was up.

"Hey Con-rad," he drawled in his Western speech, "the last time we met I never really found out what you *do*."

Conrad started. "Do?"

Conrad folded his hands and meditated into his stomach. Gabriel looked reproachful and more miserable than ever. Tony Valentine absently began to sing one of his old South Sea sailor's songs, which floated silkily on the surface of the jazz.

"He doesn't *do*," crooned Billy-Gene Valentine; "he *is*." Billy-Gene laughed as the ancients, long cold & clear, like ice in a bowl. His laugh cooled Hector, and reminded him of . . . *Olive?* Olive!

The record stopped, and somewhere they heard it being changed. An unusually tall Japanese woman entered, erect, serene, robed in a green silk kimono partner to Conrad's and coiffed in elaborate piled raven hair backed with a jeweled jade comb. She brought in fragile cups of tea and lit for Conrad a long straight pipe with a bowl the size of his thumb which he sucked on violently and passed with amazing carefulness to Tony. Hector comprehended the woman as one with the room; she had both created and been created by the little hidden lights in gold and green, the precious draperies, the transparent goldfish swimming silently behind a wall panel. She smiled past his ear, and slipped beyond him to an inner chamber.

A new record was coming on hard now, thumping and shrieking to a drawn-out kaleidoscope of orgasm. Tony's face revolved through weird contortions as he dug the music. And did his pants bulge? The others were watching intently. "Oh . . . oh baby," moaned Conrad Hurvey.

Perhaps Hector was already insane. But in time the pipe came round to him and when he drew on it the smoke inflated his throat with its harsh, exhilarating pull. And his limbs fell light and heavy, he relaxed, of all things relaxed, yes, fell headlong into deep calm pools, pool after pool.

Years later he heard Billy-Gene break out in a scream. His delicate face was convulsed with joy. "O fly!" he screamed. "Fly! Fly! My winged horse of the air! O fly the color of your wings your crystal wings my lovely fly, O fly come speck me I love you! O O O O Ohhhh! O your hairy leg brush against my cheek, my beauty let me drink deep from the jelly of your eyes! Let me be borne aloft in insect realms where only you can bear me!

"Look! He bears me! I ride, I ride!" Once more his musical laughter filled the room. Conrad and Tony were on their feet as Billy-Gene rode his fly in circles through the gloom.

Suddenly the laughter changed to a pitch which peeled Hector's skin from his flesh, the laugh insane & high.

"He's under my eyelid!" shrieked Billy-Gene. "Gouge me! Grind me!"

Tony and Conrad rushed for him and shook him, cursed him, slapped him.

"Pay no attention," said Conrad to Hector & Gabriel. "This has been going on all night." He slumped with his pipe and was off again into the music.

"Gabriel!" hissed Billy-Gene. "That is an evil man. Do you believe me, Gabriel? He is the incarnation of evil."

"I believe you."

"Evil, depraved, satanic. . . ."

Conrad's eyes were closed and a smile of beatitude formed upon his lips.

". . . the evil genius of art and love, the two-headed face of the basilisk. . . ."

"Ah, what a tea party!" said Tony Valentine. "Hey men! Did you cats hear the latest word from Our Leader?"

"You mean about testing the Ice Bomb?" Hector said. " 'Brave people of Greenland, we call upon you to sacrifice . . . '?"

"Naw," said Gabriel. "He means that bit about we've got to get a man on the moon before the Enemy."

"But why? But why? Do you know why?" Tony leaned confidentially. "We're gonna get our guy up there, and then we'll spray The Enemy with anthrax germs!"

"A gas, a real gas!" murmured Conrad.

"Life marches on," said Tony. "The spirit of progress. Remember when we talked about the human spirit? Go to the moon just to see what was there?"

"The human spirit!" screeched Billy-Gene. "What's the human spirit? What is it?"

"It's little pieces of God, baby brother!"

"Little pieces of God all over everywhere lover, I mean it, really. What about the Jupiterian spirit? I *care* about Jupiterians, I do man, with all my heart. What about the ant spirit and the elephant spirit? What is all this jazz about the human spirit?"

"Don't sound me, junior," Tony warned him laughing, "or I'll take you back to that place and Daddy will have to come sign for you again!"

"Daddy's there already," said Billy-Gene. "He runs the place, so there! No lover, God can't come in pieces, he's a whole hunk, I've seen Him, He takes in ants and Jupiterians and galaxies and anthrax germs. He's creamed up in the big fluffy juicy strawberry pie of things, and not just your puny human spirit. There can't be any such a thing all by itself!"

"Don't bother listening," Conrad said.

"But people can love!" said Hector.

"So can Jupiterians. Jupiterians love. Ants love. Ants love elephants. Elephants love Jupiterians. Love is something that fills up the universe, lover—you didn't invent it! Love's what dings God's dong and douches the cosmical chimney stack."

"Okay then," Hector said. "Maybe the human spirit is simply *mind*. Ants can't *think* anyway, and if they can they all think alike."

"How do you know? Anyway who cares about mind? What's mind, anyway? You got to unwrap yourself of mind if you want to take anything inside. I want to shut my eyes and feel something apart from my mind, like a rock floating through space, existing infinite in time and language. Are you with me, man? Can you make my rock scene?"

"Stop it, Billy," Gabriel said.

"Cool it," said Tony.

"*I* can!" said Conrad Hurvey. He was not smiling.

"I know you can," Billy-Gene replied.

"Crazy!" said Tony.

Then it occurred to Hector that he himself was a rock, floating through space, feeling, knowing all, stone-cold and stone-wise, diamond of diamonds.

They were suspended for a number of eons in the winding-throbbing of the music. Gravity vanished, and all exits led back into spacelessness.

Hector and Gabriel slept right through the second day in the rug on Conrad Hurvey's floor. On the second night they made three discoveries. First, from Conrad: that Tony & Billy-Gene were the illegitimate sons of one Moses Mandel and the blonde actress-mistress he had kept for many years. Then that was where Tony's ass-pinching came from! And Billy-Gene's wild laugh: *Olive's brother!* "It explains a lot, doesn't it?" said Conrad, smilingly devouring strips of raw fish. *The children of Moses! He runs the place.*

They were interrupted by a voice from the FM tuner: Our Country, working hand in fist with Dewdrop Ltd, had landed a man on the moon and brought him back again! Tomorrow he would address Congress and ride in ticker tape up New York.

After supper Hector and Gabriel excused themselves from prayers and stumbled through the ordered, darkened rooms, looking for the pissing place. They found instead a silken cradle, suspended from the ceiling by golden chains, and there, in the cradle, sleeping surrounded by scraps of velvet and foam rubber, lay Conrad Hurvey's prize possession. Hector and Gabriel stood for a moment awed at her steady, noisy breathing, and then bent and rubbed their cheeks along her downy hair.

Late on the morning of the third day Hector and Gabriel sat in their underwear in Conrad Hurvey's living room. Conrad Hurvey had put on his set of anonymous clothing and gone off to his work at the Agency. "Truth is, most people have dull jobs," he had said by way of explanation. His woman had also gone out, taking advantage of their presence to leave the baby.

Gabriel sat staring at the veins in the Burmese-ash coffee table. There was nothing in this world he cared about. Conrad's woman had looked at his tea leaves the night before and declined to give a fortune. Nor was Hector feeling any better. By now neither of them felt any emotion about the world they had fled from, and they would have preferred even the old anxiety.

"You know what?" Hector said. "I feel as though I've been subjected to a series of living rooms. I ask how to live and they show me living room after living room."

He went and threw open the shutters, but no light came into the room. Three feet from the window there was the wall of another luxury apartment building. The part in front of Hector was made entirely of white glazed brick, but by sticking his head out the window and twisting his neck he could see where the brick stopped and a sheen of glass began. Behind the glass, cream plush curtains were drawn.

Hector watched for a minute or two as Gabriel traced the veins in the table with his bare toes.

"Hey!" said Hector. "Look, dammit, I ask how to live and instead I get rooms opening into rooms! Is that all there is to life?"

"That's not life," Gabriel answered. "Just marriage."

"I don't believe it."

Gabriel shrugged and sighed and lay back in the furniture with his eyes closed.

"What is marriage anyway?" Hector demanded.

"Marriage is what makes men get jobs."

"What are jobs?"

"Things that don't need to be done."

"Then why do them?"

"For the sake of your children."

"For the sake of your children WHAT?"

"Why you ungrateful brat!" shouted Gabriel, springing up. "You think you're a star boarder or something? Talk to your mother like she was dirt! You're spoiled that's what, I see that now. Think everything is a one-way street—we give, you take. Well that's coming to a stop. All that's coming to a stop RIGHT THIS MINUTE! From now on there's going to be some discipline in this house! From now on we're going to know where we stand! Yes somewhere along the line we made a mistake, but no more, no siree! God, how sharper than a serpent's tooth is the something-something of an ungrateful child! Come here you little bastard: take that & that & THAT!"

Gabriel hit at Hector four or five blows, then fell back into the furniture laughing & crying in a minor way. Being his father could only give him that dilute emotion halfway between pathos and farce.

"Okay," said Hector sadly, "if that's the way you feel I'm leaving and I don't guess I'll be coming back."

He had started this reply as part of the routine, but having said it he was shocked. It was exactly what he had said to his own parents four years before, when at seventeen he had walked out of the house, gotten into his bonus convertible, and set off across the country to go to college. He had said it in that same tone of smiling sadness and then gone out and turned on the ignition and forgotten it until that very moment. He remembered now it was in the early evening when the sun was bathed in baby pink on the rim of the Pacific and the shadows of the gigantic California eucalyptus trees were stretching out a chilly blanket across the hills. The absurd pinkness, the absurd shadows, the absurd titanic scale of the land he was driving through deprived him of whatever human emotion he might have felt, and he drove back away from the sun with only a vague absence of something in the back of his brain. Not loss: you can't lose something that was never there. You can hardly know you miss it, except by the lacking in your own nature. It wasn't until the night got blue-black and the stars came out that Hector had been able to resuscitate his dreams of the learning and companionship he would find on the old historic coast.

Hector walked to Central Park and rented a bicycle from a small shop on Central Park West. The man raised the seat and handlebars as far as they would go but still Hector's knees were cramped as a grasshopper's. Instead of riding the bike around the park, he headed downtown, falling off occasionally when brushed by cars and twice almost losing his life. He had not ridden a bicycle since he'd gotten his driver's license, but it did not seem worthwhile to concentrate when he was so distracted by the textures of the old buildings and the strangely lavish cornices of tenement houses. He rode down Broadway and turned left and rode through the Lower East Side. He dismounted at a glassed-in candy counter and stood on the sidewalk drinking a sweet dose of egg cream and watching the people. Once more he was struck & bitter by how different they were from Californians: empty friendliness was bad enough, but these people were so far gone they couldn't even look back. Here & there he saw an immigrant who had never imagined not being poor, and these he could like, though he had no way of speaking to them. But most of the faces were subway faces, grey and set in bitterness, called forth from their normal scheming funk only by the noise of their children, which made them strike out. The children tried to shake free from their parents, played savagely, musingly, tenderly, exhaustingly, brilliantly, noisily, dirtily, with bottle caps and rubber balls and chalk and tin cans. They were desperately alive yet, and beautiful, but in automatic distrust of adults they turned from Hector's advances. Hector wanted to melt into the concrete: he knew they must be right. Some of the teenagers looked at him and sized him up. They were top dogs, toughest of all, bright and hard, hair set in glossy helmets, bodies clothed tight in shiny black armor. They jeered at each other instead of talking, poked testingly rather than touch, and swaggered boys and girls alike as though the whole mocking city were about to jump up their assholes.

Only the bums, in their snot shit & blood encrusted overcoats, only they approached Hector, and they talked freely, though they had long since protected themselves from the possibility of communication. The fourth bum was inspired: "I'm from Seattle!" he cried, putting his arms up on

Hector's shoulders. "Seattle the sky high as all outdoors high as God high as old El Greco Toledo Seattle, my son, Seattle!"

"What was that about El Greco?"

"Listen, buddy, let me tell you. The days are long and the nights are long. You got no idea. You think you're tough doncha? College man doncha? Old man be pushed around 'cause he's stupid! Well I'm as good. I'm as good as the next and you want trouble. . . ."

He tried to swing at Hector and started to fall. Hector caught him. The man was laughing in his face and staring with huge eyes. The stench and the feel of him were unbearable. Hector shoved him a dollar and tried to leave but the man grabbed Hector's hand in his own and shook it and laughed. The hand was filthy, scabby and covered with greasy callouses. People were gathered silent around them, watching. Hector wrenched free and rode away on his bike, while the old drunk shouted "I'm from the West you hear me the West!" and children ran screaming a block beside him poking sticks into his spokes.

Hector rode deeper, pulled deep air into his lungs, and after a while was able to admire the afternoon sun in the infinite crossings of fire escapes. When he got to the Municipal Building he dismounted and carried his bike onto the concrete island which leads to the ramp for pedestrians crossing Brooklyn Bridge. There was a sign at the bottom of the bridge that said "No Bicycles or Photographs Allowed," and Hector's reaction was *who? who says? But what's the use?* He left the bike lying there.

The webbing of the bridge arched over him in the blue sky like a cathedral. The wind was cold as the Atlantic Ocean, and turning his back to it, Hector saw Manhattan lying in the sun a smoking scattered toytown.

The bars disappeared. For three hours Gabriel had sat motionless in the furniture studying three faint bars of light on the far wall, watching as they slid imperceptibly from one end of the room to the other, and then within the space of five minutes disappeared, as though a hand of shadow had erased them from left to right.

If the key was anywhere, it was in the bars, but there wasn't any key. The longer he sat the more he knew that nothing made any difference.

Then the baby let out a cry, and he got to his feet and found he had made a decision. He laughed because the decision was not the key and made no difference, and yet he had made a decision and would act. Acting: that was the important thing. As long as he kept on acting he could forget his nothing-self and be anyone he liked.

Before he could get to the baby, the Hurvey's custom telephone began to sing an aria from *Aida*. Perhaps it was that glorious bitch Sylvie Calvin, and he could tell her to go straight to hell; more rationally it might be his mother, in which case he would pretend to be Mrs Hurvey and speak exclusively in Japanese.

It was Hector Bloom, calling from the police phone on Brooklyn Bridge.

"How are you?" Hector wanted to know.

"Fine," said Gabriel. "I'm cutting out."

"Where to?"

"I'm gonna go right now buy a ticket to Central America. Heard on the radio there's a new revolution broken out which. . . ."

"Won't last!"

"I know it won't last, man! What lasts? But dig there's a lot to do. Like cats to be fed, cats to be killed, a new government to make. . . ."

"Which will be like the old government."

"Sooner or later, OK so what? But right now they're burning up churches, & getting rid of rotten dictators & secret police & fat landowners. And all that's good, dig? When they start something new maybe I'll help make it a little better. And then when they start like buttoning down their collars and having committee meetings and telling people what to write and sending feelers to Washington & also to the Enemy, like I'll just split & move on. You know?"

"And what difference will it make?"

"I don't know, man, I'm not big enough to think about things like that. All I know is there's going to be a moment at the beginning when there's like action, dig? and men are clean and burn old shit and that's good. If they really care there's not a thing they leave standing, not one square stone on top of another. So maybe it does make a difference, man, you know things just can't be as bad as they were before!"

"Yeah?" drawled Hector. "If things aren't a goddam sight better in about five minutes they're gonna be a goddam sight worse!"

"Because look," Gabriel said. "We can live now. Really we can. Forget the necessity jazz. Because there's just no fucking point in scrapping for a loaf of bread anymore, because we know how to make plenty for everyone in the whole fucking world! We throw it away, man!"

"But if everyone can get bread that's all the more reason why someone wants up on top to eat cake. Why? Why not? He knows he's got to die. And when your lobotomized engineers build you a shiny new proto-neutronic cake maker, you can go right out and turn millions of little people into cake flour. And ain't that worse than it ever was before?"

"So what am I gonna do?" cried Gabriel. "I'm not responsible! I can't curl up and die! I gotta live, man!"

"Shit!" said Hector. Then after a while he said, "Don't listen to me. I don't know a damn thing about politics."

"It's really true. You talk in images. You're naive."

"Yeah but look, I guess this means you won't graduate."

"What does that mean?"

"Nothing."

"Well man. . . ."

"Shit!" Hector said. Neither of them knew what to say. "I guess I just want you to stick around," Hector said finally.

"Yes. I know what you mean."

"It's nice up on the bridge here," Hector said. "Lots of space."

"Don't go jumping off now man."

"Never thought of it."

"Like I know you want that broad, but you might be surprised how you'll feel if you just let her go. I did."

"Yeah. But it's not the same. I'm hanging up."

"Look man," said Gabriel. "Look, I mean . . . let us not take any shit, brother."

"Right," said Hector laughing. "Good luck, that's all I can say to you."

"Good luck."

But instead of feeling better Gabriel began to panic. It was he who had always been tempted to make the big jump. He began to wander aimlessly through room after room of Conrad Hurvey's apartment, looking for something. Whatever it was, it was not in any of the rooms. Perhaps it had been in the bars of light, but they were erased now. There was nothing left to do but leave the house and pick up his plane ticket. But before he did that he had to find something. If only he weren't afraid of flying. He was thrilled out of his wits to be up in the air but at the same time he wanted out right away. They flew very high these days, beyond gravity. Suppose one got lost from the earth? The thought of all that space made him shiver.

He was hungry and opened the legs of the huge white sanitary refrigerator. On either side of him lay morsels and snatches and ounces and bunches of palatal delight. Yet not a single bit of it was what he hungered for. The thing, the one thing. He had to have it before he could leave.

He tore through the rooms again, this time shifting furniture, flipping rugs, tearing apart beds and rummaging through drawers and closets. Nothing. In despair he went to the bathroom and stood there washing his hands over and over.

From the window came a sound faint as the bars of sunlight. Music, faint music. Gabriel ran and threw open the living room shutters and looked out but saw only the white wall in front of him. And the music was louder; it was blaring music, with the thump of drums. He ran into the master bedroom and threw open the shutters there and was hit in the face by a blast of late-afternoon orange sunlight. And music! Band music, a band was passing beneath him in Fifth Avenue, led by a van of police motorcycles and a covey of high-bouncing gold-hatted baton twirlers!

Peering out and looking down the Avenue, he saw a parade stretching back as far as he could see. It was the parade for our man on the moon. Loyal New Yorkers had flooded Fifth Avenue from one end to the other to see the man who had beaten the Enemy and done Our Country proud. Thousands of tons of scrap paper floated through the air, some of it settling now in Gabriel's hair, and twenty blocks away the newly-famous Colonel himself was moving slowly forward in an open Cadillac. Despite everything the police could do, the Colonel was being mobbed. Every faceless face in the city suddenly wanted a piece of his smile, a kiss, a fragment of his flesh. All that could be seen of the Colonel was a nest of clean-blond crewcut hair floating in a sea of tangled bodies, the skin showing through on top just as it did on the heads of Hector's teammates.

Something was beginning to break loose inside Gabriel. As he reeled back into the bedroom, his eye caught the front page of a morning tabloid thrown on a nearby chair. LET THE EAGLE SCREAM! screamed the thick black headline. And then the editorial:

. . . Ever since the Enemy sent up his first satellite, a horde of double-dome thinkers, writers and commentators have been telling us that Our Country has become a second-class nation.

We doubt that a majority of Americans ever took this stuff seriously.

But for those who have let themselves be duped concerning the power, glory and potentials of Our Country and its people, the moon triumph should be a tremendous boost in the morale.

The fact is we have the greatest country God ever put on the face of this green earth in all recorded history, and the most vigorous, creative and courageous people.

Let's all just realize that truth, and give the horselaugh to anybody who says it isn't so.

Gabriel galloped up and down Conrad Hurvey's long hallway on all fours braying like a horse. Then he jumped up on top of the refrigerator and gave the scream of the mighty bull eagle and beat his wings. He ran inspired to the window. The Colonel was now only nineteen blocks away and the people beneath were beginning to get hysterical. The air was dense with paper. Gabriel grabbed the first thing at hand, the silken blue robe Conrad Hurvey had left on his bed. The people below were too excited to notice that one out of every thousand particles descending in the next three minutes was a piece of blue silk. For the Colonel was only eighteen blocks away!

Gabriel ripped the silk bed sheets and threw them, then the clothes from the drawers: lovely pastel shirts, stretch socks, linen hankeys, filmy black panties, size 30-C brassieres, and a jingling garter belt. Gabriel pulled one nylon stocking over his head and committed the rest to immortal glory. Then the closet: Italian suits, damask sport jackets, evening gowns, suspenders, tuxedoes, foulard ties (foulard by foulard), riding clothes. A box of cashmere sweaters, torn into fluff and floating in the air like dandelion seeds. For good measure: shoes, for all occasions, a good many of them. The shoes may have hurt, especially the spike heels, but from above they seemed gently absorbed in the struggling, undulating mass below. The Colonel was fourteen blocks away.

Gabriel came from the living room with an armful of books. At first he ripped open their leather bindings and sent flakes of first-edition parchment spinning on the tide. But when the Colonel came within twelve blocks, Gabriel waxed impatient, and was content merely to sow the books one by one, discovering that if he held them back up they would puff open in the air, and drift down like parachutes. When he ran out of books, he sailed out phonograph records. These went unnoticed in the midst of men throwing caps, though perhaps the China plates did not. While the Colonel moved from ten to nine blocks away, Gabriel threw every loose object left in the house—silverware, ash-

137

trays, clocks, plant pots, food, medicine, and so forth. He poured liquids on the mob and peppered & salted them. As the Colonel crossed the intersection exactly nine blocks up the Avenue, Gabriel sent the Oriental rugs billowing out and watched them flop down enclosing a score of close-packed struggling heads. Then he began the heavy work of demolishing the furniture.

He started with the stereophonic hi-fi set, ripping the speakers from their hidden recesses and smashing them into splinters. He sent down the turntable, amplifier, pre-amp and tuner in a shower of nuts, bolts, knobs and tubes. With a meat cleaver he demolished the heavier furniture, some of which came apart quite easily, like the teak-wood dressers, but the rest—the old oak chest with stout wooden pegs in place of nails, for instance—took more extensive labor. The refrigerator proved indestructible, and since he lacked the strength to move & throw it whole, he settled for dismantling its motor and distributing its coils. Most enjoyable of all was the cushier furniture that had so utterly seduced and confounded him for the past three days. He tore out handful after handful of foam rubber, which stayed suspended in air until they had accumulated enough confetti to come plunging down like snowballs. Inspired, Gabriel went back to the refrigerator and made a few snowballs.

With the Colonel a mere two blocks away, Gabriel found himself nearly alone in the apartment. He went looking, but there was nothing of significance left. He didn't see the oil paintings and tapestries on the walls, because in his state he mistook them for the walls themselves.

The Colonel's blond head was bobbing just one block away, and Gabriel had nothing fitting to deposit upon it. But just then he heard a horrible cry, and dashing through a previously-unopened door, came into the nursery, and found himself confronted with the gold-suspended cradle. Gabriel stood, the baby howled, and the noise outside grew loud as the blast of a rocket. Did he dare?

The symbology was too much for Gabriel. In a burst of resolution he snatched the child from the cradle, ran to the window and drew back his arm. The angel-head was right below, right on target.

With his drawn-back hand, Gabriel felt two things. First, on his palm, a delicious wetness. Second, on his wrist, the child itself holding on with both hands and feet for all it was worth. Gabriel's sensuality saved him. His senses, intensified to the snapping point by his hour of ripping all the most delicate substances known to man, kept him from an act which would have utterly unstrung him, undone him, and poisoned the few short hours remaining to him on this earth. He felt the wet, felt the grip, and right in the middle of his unstoppable insanity he was hit as with a lightning bolt by the thought that this was *not* an object, no matter what its parents thought, this was a child, a human being, a life. And it was holy.

He changed the child before he left, and kissed it several times upon its belly. He was amazed at how little it took to make it happy. He gave it its bottle to hold and fled through the service entrance just as the police were breaking down the front door.

Chapter 13

Hector sat down on a bench on the long boardwalk above the traffic on Brooklyn Bridge and stayed there until three o'clock in the morning. When he turned his eyes away from the dead city behind him, he started to watch the people passing, watched them coming, passing and going, and tried to think what they were thinking. That would have been better than thinking nothing at all, which was impossible, or than thinking what he was thinking, which was inescapable.

For hours he stared down between the cables and girders and into the water below. He was not distracted by the traffic whipping by in between. He watched the ripples in the water that the wind blew, watched the waves when boats passed, watched the exchange of reflections and the darkness which began to reach up from under until it captured the surface and the waves at last flickered yellow in the solid blackness. All this while he was thinking of Olive, and his love for Olive, who fled to him and from him and who no longer wished to love him but somehow maybe loved him still. And of himself, and what he might have been were he not what he was. And what he still might be. He had thought before it was the basketball that marked off a separate part of himself, a part that had to be killed before the rest of him could form a whole and grow. And the only way to kill it was to win a victory he could enjoy, which was by definition impossible, since he could enjoy nothing until he became whole. Not even Olive. He had wanted her and he had had her, but he had not ever really enjoyed her. He had not had her right. She should have been his and freely given of her love. It was her love, not just herself, he wanted, as he had always wanted everything he could not have.

She loved him but she held back her love. She would not risk it. Perhaps he could force her to risk it, but surely he would lose what little he had.

Clearly he was destroying himself, and he knew it but couldn't stop. It was all made so easy. His world was narrow, stiflingly narrow, and yet he knew no alternatives. He honestly faced up to all the questions, and asked them ruthlessly over & over, but they were the wrong questions. Round & round he went: you need new questions before you can get new answers.

It appeared, however, that for the time being Hector would survive. He didn't know why. Perhaps because he had a sense of humor, and therefore his thoughts began to bore him and he could allow himself to be charmed and calmed by the water. Perhaps life just wasn't tough enough for him.

He stood up and saw the stars through the webbing of the giant bridge and far out over the ocean. The moon popped up from the sea and struck a path across the waters. You could walk that path like a glory road if you had the courage. The road began beneath him, where the waters flowed under the bridge, and there all around were the billion light-points of New York City, which seemed alive now and hopeful, lights flickering like stars or like souls. He was alone in a huge wind; he felt small and warm in the midst of vastness, and thought of the bridge as the one vast place in the East, a prelude to the vastness of America which lay in the prairies and mountains and rivers beyond the Mississippi.

It looked like he was going to go back and go on. He didn't know what else to do for the moment. The situation was unfinished, and if he went back and finished it the finishing would present him with a logical direction. He knew that if he left in the middle he would have to go through the whole thing again and again, acting it out with whatever materials were available until he brought it to a conclusion and could go on from there. It seemed things would turn out badly, and that was a thought he could not bear—yet he did not doubt his own survival. He thought he would last forever, because he was new enough to assume that the bridge and the sea would last forever.

And so he plunked down along the boardwalk, splashing his feet in moonlight and looking for a white whale to leap out of the water and sail over his head.

He waited in Brooklyn Bridge station to take the IRT uptown and retrieve his car. When the train came he was surprised to see so many people inside. The subways of New York are always stocked with people: these were night workers going home, early morning workers going to work, and others like Hector going nobody knows where but nonetheless up & going. The conductor must have been working all night; he came into the car and dozed between stops. The door to his little compartment was open, and as Hector passed by, he saw the loose microphone. Stepping quickly inside the booth, he switched on the mike and announced: "Next stop, 42nd Street, all pederasts and poltergeists off please. Change for a quarter and a half-dollar. Next stop after that Coney Island, and I want to warn you that a squad of red radical rapists will be getting on the train there."

"It's me."

                    "Oh. Oh. Hello."

"I want to talk to you."

                    "Hello, Aunt Hilda."

"Aunt Hilda my speckled ass!"

                    "I really can't talk now darling; we're just about to have lunch."

"Look I just got back; I haven't slept; I want to see you."

                    "But guess what Auntie. I have some wonderful news."

"If you can meet me say yes or no with your first word."

                    "No, that's not it, silly."

"Tonight then. Say yes. You've got to see me this once and be honest and say what we feel! Say yes, you haven't any choice."

                    "No listen, Aunt Hilda, I'll give you a hint. I saw the doctor today."

"Screw Aunt Hilda and screw your whole lousy runaround! Put your husband on the phone and I'll tell him it's Hector Bloom and you're coming with me and not coming back till you damn well please!"

"I'd love to help you my dear, I meant to, but really I can't just now. It's just impossible darling. You see the doctor told me today I'm pregnant."

". . . . ."

"Oh yes, yes isn't it? Morton & I are very very happy."

". . . . ."

"Oh thank you Auntie, thank you darling oh thank you you darling you're a perfect darling and your scatterbrained niece will always love you yes thank you I feel so silly you understand don't you yes but you can't really understand how I feel but you are a darling you know that honestly yes we're very happy we're going to give it a beautiful long Hebrew name and I'm just positive it's going to be a boy!"

"Grug."

"Yes, yes I know, Aunt Hilda, and really it was a marvellous surprise, you know there was no real reason for it, mathematically that is."

144

"WHAT!"

"But we're very very happy about the whole thing and we're going to be very very happy."

"What are you trying to tell me?"

"Yes, that's right. But I have to go now dear. You understand don't you?"

"You're damn right I understand! That child is mine! Yours and mine!"

"That's sweet of you to offer, dear, but it really doesn't make a bit of difference. You see there's nothing you can do for Morton & me right now. We're really quite set. We're perfectly comfy."

"You're perfectly out of your mind! That child's mine and you're coming with me!"

"Um-hmn. I'm sorry dear, it was sweet of you to call and ask, but I don't think now's the time for me to undertake new things, do you? Much as I'd like to help."

"I'm coming right over."

"Well goodbye now dear."

"You hear me? I'm coming right over & get you the hell

out of there!"

"But there's no need darling. Besides we're leaving now you see. We'll have to eat in a hurry and run without even doing the dishes."

"Just tell me straight: is that my child?"

"Yes dear, I'm afraid so. But there's really no need for you to worry your head over it, you know. Everything's perfectly normal. Thousands of other couples have had the same experience and I'm sure Morton & I will manage all right. We always have."

"Does that mean you don't love me?"

". . . . ."

"You can't say it, can you?"

". . . . ."

"You love me but you're scared, isn't that it?"

"No dear that's wrong and I really have to run now. Everything's fine and I don't want you to worry about a thing. . . ."

"You!"

"Bye-now!"

"You! Do you know what you are?"

(A click and empty space.)

He reeled from the booth.

Do you know what you are? Do you know what you are? Do you know what you are what I are what you are going to be very very really quite nothing happy sorry all right really real perfectly positive comfy all right beautiful normal thousands of thousands of couples experience perfectly beautiful the same happy nothing that's wrong I really have to I really have to manage you understand impossible don't you you understand what you are what I am what we are were going to be?

("*I'm just positive it's going to be a boy!*")

Two hours later Luther Nixon searched the little room behind the boilers in the gym and found Hector Bloom sitting in his closet.

Hector sat cross-legged among the shoes, absorbed in the wall just three inches in front of him. The sudden light did not disturb him, and when Luther Nixon prodded his shoulder, he sprang up and clutched Nixon close by the collar and pulled him feet dangling right into his red-hot eyes.

"AND ONE MORE MUTILATED BOYCHILD ENTERS THE GAME!" roared Hector, and in one furious blast threw Luther Nixon across the room out the door and flat with a thunk against a hot iron boiler.

But then Hector was obliged to gather up the lad, to put him on Gabriel's vacant-forever bed and wash his face for him, and while waiting for him to revive, gradually begin to focus on the subject before him—one single, battered, pathetic specimen, and that only. . . .

About half an hour after young Luther Nixon came to and stumbled away, there was a knock on Hector's door and in

147

came Richard Calvin and Morton Solomon together. Calvin was looking unruffled but Personally Disappointed; Morton Solomon's narrow face was twisted in a smile half-sarcastic, half-apologetic.

"When will you ever learn?" opened Richard Calvin. "When will you *ever learn?*"

"When will you ever teach me?"

"I'll teach you one thing right away. Do you know what day this is?"

"Saturday!"

"Any special Saturday?"

"If it's the first Saturday of Lent I'll gladly give up this whole conversation."

"I'll tell you what Saturday this is, young man."

"I wish you would."

"This is the Saturday of the Big Game. Remember?"

"Zounds! You're right!"

"The Really Big Game, the one you have to win to get into the National Championships. You lose, you're out, and if you don't pick up the publicity you'd get from playing before a national audience, the pros can hire you for a song. If they want you, that is. Never mind *what* song! Now there's a pro scout on campus today, and I have a feeling he'd be pretty disappointed to find that your way of preparing for the Big Game was to run away, missing your practice *and* imperative class sessions, too, I might add. *And* without leaving the slightest word as to where you were going or whether you'd return! You can't solve anything by running away, Hector."

"I'm sorry," said Hector manfully. "You can deduct it from my scholarship."

"Never mind the smart answers," said Richard Calvin sternly. "Now Morton is here in his capacity as Dean of

Men to say something to you, and if you know what side your bread is buttered on, you'd better pay heed."

"It's buttered on the kitchen-floor side, isn't it?" asked Hector, to make sure.

"Um, listen Hector," began Morton Solomon, looking uneasily over Hector's shoulder. As a rule Dean Solomon avoided direct reprimands, and he had the grace to be uncomfortable. "Well look": Solomon said, and it was evident to Hector where the discomfort didn't come from: Oh what a way he might have to cut the conversation short! *He doesn't know! He just doesn't know. He's uncomfortable, but he'll never have to be any more uncomfortable. It's his function that bothers him, not me. Olive will keep him from that, and how safe it will be for her!*

". . . Um, I get the impression you're not listening to me, Hector," Morton Solomon was saying.

"Yes I am: you were saying you talked to the President."

"Um, ya. Well, President Wollop was pretty disturbed about this whole matter. Said you've strained our patience more than once. Said something about this being the last straw."

"I'll vouch for him, Morton!" put in Richard Calvin. "He'll straighten out if I have to beat him straight, and you needn't laugh at that, Hector."

"Well you know his friends on the faculty have really protected him quite a bit all along," said Dean Morton Solomon. And here he couldn't resist a word of wisdom: "You know, Hector, do you really think your problems are so earthshaking that they should cause this much commotion for so many people?"

"In fact, I really don't have any problems, do I?"

Morton Solomon laughed a tight little laugh over Hector's left shoulder. "Why not take it easy?" he suggested.

Solomon shrugged, helpless, irritated, trying his best. "You're young. There will be plenty of real issues to fight for."

"Take it easy, but take it!" Hector said.

"You young people are so serious these days. You're old and careful. That's why you're so apathetic about politics. You're young fogies."

"We should relax and have fun, until we're old enough to know the True Tragedy of Life. Then we can become Deans."

Solomon was offended. "Well, that's life," he replied grimly.

"No," said Hector. "That's death."

"Well speaking of death," said Solomon, "do you realize that the Nixon boy was treated down at the infirmary just now for a mild concussion?"

"You can deduct it from my scholarship . . . ," mumbled Hector.

"You can thank the Lord you're a basketball star," said Richard Calvin, "or you'd be getting arrested for assault and battery this very moment!"

Hector fell to his knees. "Thank you O Lord!" he prayed. "Thanks for protecting the weak and the meek and for making it so easy to get into heaven!"

"Well I'll be God-damned!" said Dean Solomon. "Hector why are you all of a sudden so God-damn obnoxious? . . . I'm only doing my job," he muttered.

Now that Hector came up only to Richard Calvin's collarbone, Dr Calvin started shaking him. "Hector! This is no joking matter!"

Hector twisted free and stumped on his knees down the hall to the men's room, where he stared at himself in the mirror. *The eye a little bloodshot, but nothing to be ashamed of. Note how brazenly, how soulfully, it looks back at you. And even in times of asperity, a twinkle. Small wonder the tragic spouse of the Intelligence Coordinator was bewitched. Yes, there it is a definite twinkle! Only sign of life there is. Man: eyes like that, soul like that . . . worth all the Luther Nixons and Morton Solomons that ever lived, mixed together and compressed into a can of tuna fish. Why man, life should be a JOY!*

Some chest-beating and a moderate roar out the window, a dozen chin-ups on the toilet door, and Hector was as good as . . . ever? When he came back to the Real World, Morton Solomon had gone, but Richard Calvin was patiently waiting, and clutching Hector's arm, hoisted himself on tiptoe to deliver some sound advice.

"Listen Hector, the word from the President is that you'd better come through tonight, do I have to say more? The Office of Student Personnel has enough on you to bounce you out and keep you out of every school in the country. And bar you from pro basketball, too. I'm going to go now and keep that pro scout company until game time. In the meantime your teammates are already eating at training table. They're pretty down on you, Hector, and if I were you I'd make a little speech of apology."

"OK," said Hector. He slapped Richard Calvin on the seat of his pants and headed for the Athletic Dept's private dining room. Yes, the others were already there, slurping their wheat germ, and when Hector entered no one but Goose Jefferson even so much as nodded. Fighting Coach Jack Bullion sat at the head of the table like a white Buddha, and spake not a word.

It was time for Hector to make his address. He cleared his throat.

"Fellow employees," he began, "lend me your ears. I

come to bury Hector, not to praise him. The evil that men do lives after them, the strontium 90 rots apart their bones: So let it be with Hector. The noble President hath told you we better come through tonight, or publicity will be at a grievous fault. And I say unto you, yea verily, realize the consequences of a defeat!"

"Talk like a man!" yelped Rod Jellop.

"Okay men," said Hector, leaning down confidentially. "This is it. If we don't win, the world will split in half, longitudinally, in two equal parts. If we do win, the world will split horizontally. Both halves will fall smack on the floor of the universe, buttered side down."

A few rose, as if to leave the table.

"Wait!" Hector cried. "In case of a tie, the world will split diagonally, each team falling on a separate-but-equal half!"

This was too much for Goose Jefferson, who began surreptitiously giggling into his honeyjuice—his secret self bubbling up through the arteries irrepressible.

"Jefferson!" Hector snapped. "Stop that at once! You know respectable Negroes aren't supposed to laugh!"

Immediately Hector drew himself a tableful of nasty scowls from the spontaneously-formed Coach's Committee for Liberalism & Tolerance. Goose had to leave the table with a laughing jag, but his eyes informed Hector that he had broken the unspoken code, and might not be forgiven.

"All right," bluffed Coach Bullion. "Just a case of pre-game jitters. Let's calm ourselves down now."

His soothing speech melted the butter on their steaks. When Goose Jefferson was able to return to the table, Coach Bullion informed him, "Thomas, I want you to know that Bloom's wisecracks represent no one on this team but himself."

"That goes for me too," Hector said.

"Bloom," said his coach, with the air of one breaking a long and meaningful silence, "I hope for your sake you play well tonight. The rest of us kinda think we're entitled to something just for putting up with you."

Big leer at this point from a pale and dramatically head-bandaged Luther Nixon.

There passed an entire minute of soundless satisfaction. Hector looked from one man to the next without engaging a single pair of eyes.

"I was never a man for pregnant silences," he said at last, "so if any of you has a complaint about the way I've treated him man to man, let him speak out RIGHT NOW!"

Hector was standing, eyes blazing. The table was silent as a tomb.

"Goddammit I have treated you as EQUALS!"

He walked straight out and stormed down the back hill of the campus, so furious he did not know where he was. *But you're* NOT *my equals*, he thought, *not in a million years*. Tears of rage in his eyes. *I will win that game I will win it win it win* . . . but how deeply he hated the thought of playing!

Chapter 14

He went to Morton Solomon's house and walked through the front door without knocking. Olive was back in the kitchen, and when she saw him coming gave a little gasp and stood tensely with her back up against the refrigerator.

"Here I am," said Hector. "Won't you come with me please?"

She shook her head.

"Olive, you're the mother of my child. I want you to come and be with me."

He could see her bracing herself. She looked like anyone but a mother. With her apron on, with her long hair strewn, with her wide eyes and her frightened mouth, she looked like a small confused girlchild, who wouldn't budge off the spot till she was sure she weren't being tricked.

Hector smiled as his heart sank. He crooned:

Will you won't you will you won't you
  will you join the dance?
Will you won't you will you won't you
  won't you join the dance?

But she would not could not would not could not would not join the dance. She would not could not would not could not could not join the dance. She wasn't ready.

Hector went and sat on a stone. There was a crust of dirty snow on the ground, and while he sat there, snow began to fall once more, dirty, tiny snow from a lead-slate sky. The cold began to seep up through his shoes and from the stone into himself and back again. At last he had a thought and it was that he should go but he could not give the command which would set his limbs in motion. He was calmer; the utter greyness of the place had entered into him and sat inside him, turning him part stone, part man, alone and growing colder in a grey woods with grey-black dying trees beneath a grey sky chipping off and falling. In the background a grey stone library looming, stone upon stone, reflected stone sky from stone-plate windows.

A bar of light fell across his knees. He had the shameful feeling that from some one of those slate-shining library windows a woman large in heart and in beauty was watching him and loving him. His yearnings filled him with self-contempt. *What more, what next?* Even the basketball players must love him. In that respect they were truly his equals: he did not despise them any more than he despised himself.

His legs were moving him on a long, strength-sapping walk, feet performing hole after hole in the decaying snow. He wanted to wear himself down, wear down the fire that might spark alive in his chest and consume him, wear himself passive and helpless in face of the event he dreaded, which he had to win, would surely win, though only losing would finish him up and throw him in the way of some path he could enjoy.

Chapter 15

⟶ Hector sat in the lockerroom, putting on his home uniform. His face was relaxed and his eyes were glazed and unfocused. He was singing to himself. Wherever he was, he was out there all alone.

No gal made has got a shade
On Sweeeet Georgia Brown.
Two left feet, but oh so neat
Is Sweeeet Georgia Brown.

He was singing the ballad of the Harlem Globetrotters, but he was not thinking of basketball.

They all sigh and wanna die
For Sweeeet Georgia Brown
I'll tell you why . . .
*   I don't lie.*

It's been said she knocks 'em dead
When sheeeee lands in town.
Since she came, why it's a shame
How sheee cools 'em down. . . .

As the conductor came down the aisle taking tickets, Gabriel Reuben got up and went back to the men's room at the end of the car. When the conductor looked for him in the men's room, Gabriel had put on his stocking and left and was hanging in-between cars. As the train slowed he shut his eyes started to jump and checked. The train slowed more and Gabriel jumped and rolled down the embankment like coal going down a chute.

Everyone say Yea! The home team's were blue and white and the Enemy's red and black. *Crazy!* Hector saw open faces and upper fronts and arms up: the legs had to be tied down *or else we would have chaos and we can't have that, can we?*

They were watching the two teams shoot balls at their baskets and after a while of that everyone had to stand still while some music played. It was not Sweet Georgia Brown, but someone sexless and bluffing and so oppressive that no one listened to him anymore. Then on the sidelines while Coach talked urgent urgent and no one listened and the hands were piled tight and they broke and ran out on the floor and the tension flared up in a big blunt roar.

Gabriel cursed to see the gym all lighted up. He had to get himself cleaned. Limping he picked his way through a phalanx of sleeping cars and got into the gym through the basement door. Even in the bowels of the boilers he heard the boom of the PA: "Basket by Bloom!"

The ball had come to him far out and on the side. He dribbled looking for the pass, couldn't find a man open and checked and tripped and started to fall and on the way down heaved the ball away towards the basket where it bounced from the rim, fell off the backboard, bounced again from one rim to another, rolled around & around and fell through. It shouldn't have gone in but it did. Hector couldn't get over it. The crowd liked his sloppy luck better than any of the thousand times he had made it look easy. And he liked it best of all. The next time he just let fly from center-court and that went in too.

He had done this so often. If he lived old as Noah, he would never again in all his life have the chance to do the right thing at the right time when the chips were down for so many people. Isn't that sad?

Why have they done this to me? he thought as he did it again and they did it again, but by his own answering sensation he knew the question didn't matter for now but only the hard fact that he was what they did and they were what he did. He did not think of afterwards because he was feeling so loose and wild not thinking of now.

Gabriel did as best he could with a little alcohol and changed all his clothes but his sports jacket. He couldn't find another jacket so he decided to wear the one that shredded to pieces rolling down the embankment. He looked at himself in his shaving mirror and saw that even with the nylon stocking over his head his face had gotten torn and bruised. Still, it seemed right: the face he saw in scabs and scratches was his favorite movie of himself, the face of a born revolutionary, made to destroy and be destroyed before the dead stock exchange has time to come back to life. Because the stock exchange always does come back: eventually someone picks up the table, slaps its legs firm, restacks the scattered coins and bills, and the temple is open for business again.

And no one fucks anymore, thought Gabriel.

Hector took a rebound and crouched while three of the Enemy hung on his back slashing at the ball and hacking him on his arms and hands. Was this their idea of a beautiful game? Hector struck out savagely with his elbows . . . and had the satisfaction of sinking them in flesh.

The population of the whole town had funneled itself into the gymnasium. Gabriel marched aching through the streets and there was no one to peep out and see him. It was possible to believe himself a giant, his head poking holes in the night sky, the street his footpath, the boxy white houses empty cartons to be kicked aside by his foot. He pulled his stocking on again so as to blur the havoc he was wreaking.

Coming in and out of focus. Now he had the ball and twisted like a freight train in toward the basket shrugging off passengers right and left yes cramming it through and running back on defense fading away running for the joy of his legs on a huge blind beach with ocean CRASH . . . .

The only person left at home in the whole town . . . she opened the door and was too shocked to slam it closed again. Before her loomed a twisted bullet head, the features smeared and leering, behind her open on the couch the Magazine Beauteous, crammed generously full of sleek hip tourists and colored jungles, palm trees, castles on the Rhine, Kremlins, pagodas, gambling casinos with cut-glass chandeliers, barracudas, alligators, friendly llamas, yaks, bowing Tibetan monasteries, Japanese cameras, Italian racing cars, braces of Borzoi, frottage in Rio at festival time, the Grand Dragon of New Orleans, colored people, yellow people making shirts in Hong Kong, street whistlers in India outside the polo match where a man in a lilac turban looks at your legs, all alone just you two on the moonlit beach at Waikiki, he takes your hand atop the Empire State Building and you plunge in his embrace deep in tailored suede leaves the new fall foliage in Beautiful Brown County Indiana. Next month: An earthlight dip, on the moon. What to wear in a moonsoon. Gabriel removed his moon-gauze and revealed himself. It was he. She saw the wounds on his face, but her expression did not soften.

Hector sank a running hook-shot from the corner so graceful that were he on horseback he would have been clearly the greatest polo player in the whole blooming British Empire; but he didn't even know it, for he was in spirit a prehistoric reptile-bird skimming through the steaming swamp with leather pointed eyes alert for prey, and the shout they sent up for him was heard clear out across town to the house of Richard Calvin where Gabriel put his hands on Sylvia Calvin's hips and stared at her intently.

"What do you want?" she said, annoyed.

Blood? thought Hector, as the red stuff dripped from his nose and a manager came scurrying out on the floor with a towel. And once more he found himself back in a game.

An Enemy charged like an ancient angry mastodon, but in the nick of time everlasting Hector swiveled cleanly with his hips and sent him sailing into the background.

"Get out of heah!" she said, and Gabriel struck a red smack on her clean face.

There was a long pause for half-time. Hector lay on the training table sleeping like a baby while the trainer lovingly sealed up his fingernail scratches. "I'm going to call the po-lice," Sylvie Calvin said, and Gabriel took out a knife and cut up the telephone into molecules.

Gabriel didn't know what to say. He screamed at the top of his lungs while dancing war dance in the telephone snow. Sylvie sat stiffly tried to ignore him ignore her fright so new to her she didn't even know the name for it and hated it because it was new and she hated it and she hated him and held on tight so he would go away and leave her alone. She reached out quickly and snapped on the television but he cut that up too and flushed it down the toilet.

Why didn't she love him? Why didn't she see the magic he could do and love him?

Hector wondered that too wondered every time he came back to himself but there was no time they were going back out and Goose Jefferson came up and shook him and said, "We got to run, baby." "Why not, Goose?" demanded Hector, but Goose just shook his head; it was too late and out of his ken. Goose patted Hector shook his head and they went back out on the floor.

Gabriel held Sylvie tightly on the couch and before long he was jerking against her but she was squirming irritated crying let go and it was all humiliating his pleasure and he was so weak he toppled on the floor she falling on top and nasty shaking him saying okay now okay will you get out now?

And so on the tip Goose trapped the ball and scooped it downcourt to Hector on the run, took the return pass and whipped it behind his back to Hector all alone under the basket for a lay-in. Then they turned around and stole the pass-in got another basket and a freethrow besides. They went into a press on defense harassing those poor boys our Enemy till the shit ran down their hairy legs and their eyes sparkled with sweat and hate and their stubby hands flailed and snatched with desperate malice but the ball was gone and Hector driving, he sailed, twisted, shoved the ball up and around and shifting hands shoved it through a tangle of outthrust arms off the boards and into the basket. His own arms were rubber and ten feet long. He was hearing his own music, moving out & on to the most electric rhythm section ever convoluted together in a single brainpan.

And they hit him more than ever, in time and out of time. *Why?* She spat in Gabriel's face.

Because magic disturbs.

Magic will be investigated by a committee and held in contempt and swung by the balls until dead. Accordingly Gabriel slashed at her clothes with his knife and cut them into gorgeous swirls and crescents. She kicked at his groin, but he caught her foot and twisting her in a leglock trimmed off her rosebud-painted toenails and ate them one by one.

"You are mine!" he shouted, as she lodged kick after kick furious at a man who encroached upon her body and would not be handled or ignored. And then when she jumped up and tore away leaving him holding her ripped-out dress she turned at bay and was nauseated by the rosy glow of his palate.

She was naked and resplendent and there was nothing he could do.

Hector was resplendent and unstoppable and there was nothing they could do but go into a zone defense with one man free just for him, which was fine, just fine for his side as they worked their give-and-go and set up picks and Hector shot his jumpshot from far, far out behind the screen and the ball sailed dead in the air not-turning came down clean as a bomb through the hoop and the cords flipped their skirts and the crowd jumped for joy and came down again held in by the legs.

Gabriel lapped at her pubic zone grazing like a goat while she smoked her fingers trembling flipped through her magazine traveling straight out of her mind with the tickling nibbling finally convulsed in shameless laughter loose and losing it and terrifying herself as his volcanic breath scorched the earth where she knew no crop would grow again but what did she care my god my god stop! My God Yes! No! My God! MY GOD!

The lights came down hot through the smoke and they poured it on, flipping the ball from hand to hand running it down and down, way gone. The basket hung in the bright big as a bathtub as they shoveled in points from all over the floor. Goose took a floor-length pass from Hector and laid one up behind his back. Hector sprung for a tip-in all the way out by the foul line and batted in another on the end of a high bullet-pass. He took them past 100 all alone as he squirmed through a panicked tackle and came in on a fast break, not laying the ball up but floating with his whole forearm above the basket and stuffing it, ramming it through to the floor like a pistol shot.

Gabriel too at last came ramming like a pistol shot hot on the heels of hah the first pleasure she'd ever in her life been forced out of control into but whunk he was met with muscle closed so tight so hard he bent his subversive in half and howled to high heaven. He was Inadequate: to probe her she must be probed with a carved African fertility symbol spear and all, a sea-wave-sharp Israeli ashtray of Pharaoh's-blood red, and a white Danish coffee stirrer made from the platinum spoke of the famed Copenhagen downhill racing bike. All these she absorbed while he kept tally on her full strong thigh with his Boy Scouts of America camping knife.

"NOW!" he cried.

"NO!" she cried, and smashed him across the lung with a Colonial brass andiron.

"I'll kill you, you bitch come here!" But he did not want anymore to kill her and he crushed her in his arms and kissed her very sweetly and gently forgetting all about the knife in his hand and genuinely surprised and sick when he felt the sudden gush of blood down his throat.

It ended up with Goose Jefferson dribbling in circles, the ball an eighth of an inch off the floor beneath his huge pale palm like a pea, magically eluding the lungers who grabbed around him like five angry bumpkins for their money back.

And the crowd at last pulled loose and spilled across the floor and crushed them close in ecstasy forgetting and forgiving everything. Hector Bloom was pushed right up against Fighting Coach Jack Bullion who wanted to hug and kiss him so that Hector had to twist and finally slapped his Coach on the back so hard his teeth came out and got stomped to dust the moment they hit the floor. Goose Jefferson was captured by a platinum blonde cheerleader who embarrassed him purple squeezing up against him bouncing her tight little twat up and down and up and down as the surging crowd buggered her from behind.

Gabriel heard the noise and danced all the more wildly, danced to the sweet spirit of death to sustain him trampling down the fear that welled & trampling sprinkling the blood around the room in tiny drops that crackled on the wall like pricks of fire, like screams from thirty thousand banshee throats as Hector rode hoisted on the shoulders of the mob who would not yet lynch him not as long as he was theirs he smiling like an angel completely out of it not knowing that a famous victory was won and lost and singing FuckyouFuckyouFuckyouFuckyou into a rout-chorus so immense that his single voice was drowned deep as God's green ocean.

Chapter 16

⟶ Fresh from the Athenian victory shower Hector came up against Richard Calvin with pro scout in tow, smiling happily, daddily. Hector brushed them aside and dressed only laughing not talking to them, not answering reporters either, only smiling laughing cracking hands when people wanted to shake. Only the photographers were happy, though the reporters didn't really care. In the middle of the crush stood the pearl-striped pearl-haired pearl-brained double-breasted Director of University Publicity, passing out statements by Hector, Goose and the others that he had personally written and graph-o-pressed before the game. "Boy, were they a hustling ball club!" said Hector's statement in part. "But we had to win this one for Coach!" And so no one really cared that Hector didn't talk words. Only Richard Calvin cared, sincerely, and it was touching to see him moping about—though as he looked at Hector there was a moment when his moping gave way to fright. For Hector confronted Richard with the same weird grin that had appeared on his face at a certain point during the basketball game—for a moment, when he made that first lucky shot—then later, with his music, to stay. "Hector, for God's sake!" Richard said, and the scout said, "Listen Bloom you're great but no one's God you better get that idea out of your head right now fella if you know what's good for you in the big time!" Hector gave him a large kiss on the forehead. He was going one last time to Olive, and he was not thinking yet where to go after that. The game was over and he was still OK and the winter night air came cold in his lungs like a change of season.

Olive and Morton Solomon drove home from the game in silence, and she went inside to start coffee while he put the car in the garage. Before he got to the back door, however, Hector Bloom went in and slammed the door in his face and locked and barred it. He did the same with the front door. Through the window Morton Solomon saw Bloom confront his wife in the kitchen. Solomon was shocked; his wartime violence returned to him: in an instant he had reached up and smashed a kitchen windowpane with his hand, but there was no way to go about climbing in, and so he stood there cursing and sucking his bloody hand, torn between his need for law and his fear of leaving. With a sudden cry of decision he broke for the garage and backed out accelerating in angry bursts bruising his fender on the picket fence and swinging a furrow through the front lawn. When he got his car into the street, he shifted into forward, stalled the motor, started again, and roared off. At last Morton Solomon knew, and Hector was petty enough to be glad of that . . . though when he saw the hatred in Olive's feartight face he felt sick and angry and his love was over.

But Hector still had the habit of his love—still too young too hopeful having forced his way in to lose what he came for—and so took Olive to his heart and kissed her fiercely, and to his surprise she responded fiercely. She circled his neck and kissed him and clave herself close to him and kissed him again, again, kissed his eyes and his chin and his forehead. For she really did love him, though she did not love him enough, and she knew, he knew, that she was kissing him goodbye.

"Why did you do it?" she asked him. "Don't you know what you've done?"

He did not, or would not. "No," he said. "Why not? What else?"

"You've ruined everything," she sobbed. She sat on a tall wooden stool, forlorn, her legs dangling and her back slumping and shaking as she wept into her slender hands and the fluorescent tube shone remorselessly purple on her skin and hair.

"I don't understand," Hector said. "Why couldn't it be?"

"Because it can't, it can't it just can't, don't you see that? You say come with me but you won't take care of me!"

She went on crying into her hands but when he tried to touch her to smooth her hair she raised her head and screamed out at him hysterically.

"Get away from me! Damn you let me alone! You great big clumsy bastard! What more do you want? You broke up everything I ever had! Is that enough? You want more? Oh I loathe you, I *loathe* you! . . . I want to *die!*"

And she screamed a wailing awful scream full in his face, her own face distorted and gaping like a child in pain who will not be fooled or comforted because he knows pain hurts and big people lie. Hector stood helpless, while from inside him his own child's face wailed back at her.

Chapter 17

━━━━━━━━━━▶ Hector left as Morton Solomon rushed up the front walk with the policeman on the beat, hell-bent on vengeance and divorce. To keep his freedom it was necessary to knock them down and handcuff them together. Perversely he jumped into Morton Solomon's new car to make his getaway. Perhaps he wanted to show he had learned something at college: *exercises in minor irony*. He made as many turns as he could and finally headed away from the area on a backwoods road.

He snapped on the radio, and the voice of the late-evening disc jockey was heard in the car, chockfulsome of personality. "Oh yeah," said Hector. "Oh Yeah?" He drove through small upstate towns where blinking gnomes were rolling in the sidewalks for the night. *Everywhere I go I see them hide themselves.*

"Hey out there all you boys and girls in dreamland!" replied the DJ.

And then the local station cut in for some special announcements. First, the Big Game. "Big Hector Bloom poured in a record-breaking 64 points tonight, folks, as the . . . ." Then, a more chilling item—the wife of a professor found murdered: Mrs Richard Calvin!

Hector had trouble taking it in. The announcement was over before he heard the end of it and a Latin-American orchestra had come on shaking red and orange garbagecansful of music.

Gabriel! But Gabriel was back in New York! *Still, it is, it has to be.*

And Sylvie Calvin: not dead? He had pictured her living on & on, like a tree.

He still couldn't take it in. He would have had less trouble understanding that he had murdered Olive.

He switched to another station and heard the same announcement over again.

". . . left at the scene of the crime, inexplicable paper stars, pasted on the ceiling, floor, the furniture and parts of the body itself. According to investigating officials, the stars are white, and printed on each one is Old Glory, with the words, 'THE AMERICAN REVOLUTION.' There has been speculation here and in Washington that this points to a great Enemy conspiracy of which the student murderer was only an innocent dupe."

Student murderer—what student murderer? Do they know it's only Gabriel, that innocent dupe? Ah innocent dupe student murderer, stay in New York tonight: go out on Brooklyn Bridge and they'll never find you!

Hector knew he was not reacting properly. He could not believe the announcement, yet he was sure that Gabriel was the murderer and was now in mortal danger. In that case he should find him and help him, but wouldn't that be ludicrous? If he saw Gabriel would he laugh or cry? For once Hector wasn't reacting. Gabriel and Gabriel's murder had no meaning for him. He himself was fleeing with his own love killed. And it was all he could do to keep his killed love real. The thought of her with her husband: preferring her husband: soothing him: kissing her husband in his ear and whispering: having his child with her husband: it was not real. Ever since he had been driving only one thought: It's happening, *It's happening to me and there's nothing . . .* had been real in his mind. *Real?*

But she loves me! She loves me still it's happening. It's happening anyway and there's nothing . . . .

And on the radio, without warning, came a blast of God's new heaven:

> BYE BYE LOVE!
> BYE BYE HAPPINESS!
> BYE BYE SWEET CARESS!
> BYE BYE MY LOVE BYE BY-EYE
> I THINK I'M AGUNNA DIE-EYE.

O they sang like four cannonballs! Hector sat petrified. He couldn't switch them off, and so they went on, taunting him, shredding his taut nerves:

> THERE GOES MAH DARLIN
> WITH SUM-ONE NEW.
> SHE TELLS ME MISTER
> YOU'N I 'ER THREW.

Something strange was happening. Instead of coolly protecting himself against the music, Hector was letting it bounce him along, relaxing, an idiot grin pulling apart the corners of his mouth as he jingled, jangled, the imbecile rhythm pounding him back to insane prenatal days of teen-age lobotomy.

Bumbadumbadump   BYE BYE LOVE
Bumbadumbadump   BYE BYE HAPPINESS
Haayah!   HELL-LLO EMPTINESS
                     BYE-UH-BYE MY LOVE-UH
                     GOOD-BYE-UH

Hector drove stupefied, hypnotized, slamming the steering wheel with his hand, stomping the accelerator in rhythm, slam-slamming as drove up, up (and why not?) along the riverbank, heading straight out of his mind!

                     I'M THREW WITH ROMENCE
                     I'MA THREW WITH LUV
                     I'MA THREW WITH COWNTIN
                     ALLASTARS A-BUV

AnI'mtellinyew   BYE BYE LOVE
Bumbadumbadumpa BYE BY-AH LOVELINESS
Hey there!   HELL-LLO LONELINESS!
                     BY-UH-BYE MY LOVE-UH
                     GOOD-BYE-UH

                     BY-UH-BYE MY LOVE-UH
                     GOOD-BYE-UH

                     BY-UH-BYE MY LOVE-UH
                     GOOD-BYE-UH

And as the silver wirecords flashed to his right,

he knew   LUV LUV!
Bumbadumbadumpa KNEW JUST WHERE-HE-WAS
                            HELL-LLO CADILLAC
                            I'MA LOOKIN HERE FOR YEW-
                                OO
                            I'MA LOOKIN HERE FOR YEW

                            I'M SEEKIN YOU BABY
                            I'M SEEKIN MAH LUV
                            I'M SEEKIN YOU CRAY-ZY
                            ASA STARS A-BUV

anI'mtellinyew   BYE BYE LUV
Yes!   HOTHERE: BLACKADILLAC
                            HERE'S HECTOR COMIN
                            ON YA BACK

                                gooba-gook-gooba-gook-gook-googuk
                                gooba-gook-gooba-gook-gook-gook

Chapter 18

➤ Hector came out of it laughing. He had started to laugh in the nick of time. Whether his laugh will hold till old age, who can tell?

He was ready to drive all night. The important thing was to find his friend Gabriel and hold him safe. He turned tail on the beckoning Hudson and roared down from the high riverbank into the flatlands with a mammoth appetite. He stopped at a dazzlingly clean diner and ate a sirloin steak on a platter big as a truckwheel, with fried eggs and potatoes and black bread on the side and a wedge of pie and a pot of coffee for dessert. He didn't stop again until he got to Fifth Avenue, at about three o'clock in the morning.

The eye of Conrad Hurvey gleamed like blue porcelain. "Hector, baby!" He had been meditating alone in a haze of opium smoke. He took down the chain and let Hector in, proceeded to tell him how he had come home the previous night to find his wife sobbing like a blown rose in the midst of his own shattered soul-stuff. "It shook me up, you know, it cooled me," he confessed. But now that he had had time to dig it better, it was a cool scene on Gabriel's part. If Conrad had come in earlier, he would have given Gabriel a hand. Gabriel was a young cat whose noise would be heard, he was sure of that, and Hector did not tell him that Gabriel might well have blown his last big sound.

"Besides," Conrad said, "no problem, man. No sweat." His full-sleeved arm swept grandly to indicate the vista, which had been entirely reinstituted. Most of the near room was taken up by a tasteful lotus pond, in whose silent waters diaphanous goldfish twisted. Hurvey swept up a lotus blossom and held it delicately in his jade-ringed fingers. He sniffed it. "The lotus blossom, symbol of sweet forgetfulness. We have already forgotten Gabriel Reuben and his act of immaturity." With a casual motion of his wrist, he wafted the lotus blossom into the pebbled tiles of a rock garden, where a lizard slithered out and ate it.

Hector went full speed north. He arrived in the university town shortly before dawn, and spent some time driving slowly through the streets looking for Gabriel. Richard Calvin's house was roped off, and the crowd of official cars around it plus a suspicious look from the cop who waved him past reminded Hector he was driving a hot article. He drove to the gym and left the car in Coach Bullion's parking slot, then went back to the gym for a long, lovely, gratifying piss.

He was heartened to find that Gabriel had been in the room, and set off on foot to look for him on campus. Since it was dawn on a Sunday morning, he was alone, and his feet echoed coldly on the long stretches of concrete paving. The campus was foreboding in the light of this dawn. The buildings looked grey and unwholesome, like so many pieces of plumbing. Hector wondered what they could be used for. Perhaps boxes, but then the glass sides leaked tin at the corners. The campus itself had been stamped down on top of a wooded hill which could be seen for miles around and was by nature the most beautiful spot in the whole countryside. But in the four years Hector had been there, the buildings had doubled themselves, and confined all trees to nature areas. An intensive fund drive was still underway to provide for twice as many more erections, including, in the words of University President Horace Wollop, "the entire spectrum of professional schools." Dr Wollop had formerly headed the nation's largest graduate school of Public Relations, and had a keen sense of "the responsibility we owe American education. For there is no freedom without responsibility."

As he picked his way among the slabs of concrete and cinder block, Hector recalled a Christmas morning long gone when Irving Bloom had bestowed on his budding Bloom a Supersize Erector Set. Father and son had had little to do with one another, and both were nervous as Hector awkwardly bolted some of the smaller pieces into a circle of tiny doll's houses in which he pretended his friends and himself were living. This was enough to start him thinking, but seeing his father's tight hands, he knew he had to do more, and grabbing the leftover pile of flat metal beams began to lay them out end to end in two parallel lines across the rug. "Now what in God's name do you think you're doing?" his father had said. "Making a railroad," Hector had shyly explained. "See, it goes across the Rocky Mountains and over the Mississippi and all the way to New York City!" And his father had clapped his hands together and strode right through the railroad and out of the room, leaving behind a loser.

Shortly thereafter the father next door brought his son two years older than Hector and the two men went off for a beer. The boy next door was an old hand with erector sets and quickly bolted together an enormous facsimile of the Empire State Building, big as Hector himself and replete with an elevator which ran on its own tiny motor. When the boy had gone home, Hector had taken his sand pail and cut savagely into the metal structure, fighting it eventually with his hands and feet until the beams snapped and curled into emblems of his outrage. . . . As usual, the ungrateful child kept his silence when whipped. By that time an issue had been settled.

And the funny thing was, it really had little to do with his parents. He knew, even then, that the Empire State existed, whereas his circle of dollhouses and his mythic railroad were merely personal. He had simply responded, from a feeling already deep inside himself, to some force already powerful, already enormous, already unavoidable, years before he was born. Before his father was born, for that matter. His father, too, was only reacting, and Hector had long since given up blaming him.

As he walked along with his eyes open it seemed clear to Hector that certain actions were a crying-out-loud part of the scene itself, were the only way to make the scene complete, and had no more to do with what one was than Gabriel's safe New York family or Hector's own lost California family had to do with what they were. *Each in his own way, that's all, and who knows when it will stop?*

At the summit of the campus, where the entrance portal marked the university boundary and the hill sloped away into town, the curve of University Road was lined with huge brick fraternity houses, each barred in by a row of whitewashed wooden pillars. Nearby stood a white humpy building, the largest on campus, the Administration Building, "a tribute to the academic concept." As Hector walked up from the bottom of the row, he noticed that the frat houses were specially decorated. A ceremony was obviously slated for that day. Suddenly he remembered: it was the University Centennial Convocation to celebrate the Wholeness of Western Man. "Scholars, creators, and princes of industry" had been collected from all over the world to consecrate the day—in fact, he recalled that Gabriel had received instructions a month in advance to be on hand (as part of his work scholarship) to help set up a platform in the gym for ceremonies which were to take place that afternoon. Hector walked faster, thinking to cross the hill and head back down to the gym, where he hoped Gabriel would have reappeared.

As he walked, he noticed that parked in front of each house was a float, upon which stuffed figures represented the theme of the Convocation. Apparently a parade and competition had been held the day before, when he had been occupied with the Big Game: some of the floats were marked with prize ribbons. In front of the Administration Building stood the most enormous of all, the first-prize winner, and Hector stopped at the foot of it to strain back his neck and gape.

He was standing near a cleated football shoe which could well have held the entire football team. On the toe of the shoe was emblazoned in orchids the Greek letters KTΛ, standing for the sorority which had created this awesome monument to Western Man's Wholeness. From the shoe up stretched a straw-stuffed canvas statue of the University football coach, replete with a gigantic whistle of sterling silver hung from his neck and a football made of thirty-two pigskins under his arm.

Opposite the football coach towered a figure with a knarled and withered substructure, over which was draped acres of black canvas after the manner of an academic gown. Under its arm was clutched a book of symbols, and up under the black mortarboard with tassel of horsetails dangling down, Hector recognized the gleeful, wizened features of the chairman of the Practical Biology Dept, world-renowned as the father of nerve gas.

In between the football coach and the gas prof, reconciling them, so to speak, stood the mighty statue of the University President. He was clad in a dove-leather business suit made of real doves, and with his crown of platinum hair (real platinum) and his benevolent smile (elephant's tusks), he seemed the guardian angel of academic cordiality. His arms spread wide to take in the other figures, as indeed they had spread wide to embrace the entire tradition of Western thought.

After a long period of study Hector spied what appeared to be a blemish on the President's lofty nose, and his heart jumped. Then the blemish jumped, and Hector strained his magnificent eyes to be sure. He cupped his hands and began to call, but already the procession of Cadillacs was winding up from the bottom of the hill.

Gabriel had slept for several hours. Yawning now, he looked down and took pleasure in his active friend Hector Bloom so far below and full of life. Gabriel Reuben was sick and very tired, and he shuddered as the Cadillacs crept thick around the statuary, silent and evil as roaches.

Calmly Gabriel Reuben lit a cigarette, and sat there on the President's turned-up stuffed canvas nose, smoking and absently watching the smoke dissolve in the rarefied, empty air. There was really nothing to think about, and certainly no chance the roaches would ever go away. It was like in the cowboy movies Gabriel loved so well: him or them. There: he saw Hector down below bouncing up and down like a jumping bean and pointing up at him, and the others coagulating around Hector to push him away. Gabriel smoked calmly and looked far out over the rim of the horizon, where he fancied he saw green forests and jutting mountains as yet unventured upon by men. Then he reached up and put out his cigarette in the President's straw blue eye. For an instant nothing happened and from his spot climbing frantically up the President's leg Hector saw Gabriel get to his feet and stretch out his arms in a marvelous parody of freedom—and then in a flash the entire trinity was enveloped in a sheet of white flame.

And so Gabriel left this world as he had always wished to leave, by his own choice and in a conflagration. Doubtless it brought a smile to his austere angel-lips to learn that he had taken with him the nearby Hymen Hubris Hygiene Building, the Orman Rappoport Center for Public Opinion Studies, and the God Bless America Institute of Veterinary Arts.

Nearly suffocated by the coil of black smoke, Hector Bloom hacked free of the insect crush. He had fallen twenty feet into a bed of melting lilacs. He was pasted head to foot with ash, and as he stopped to free his mouth and nose and eyes he saw a white butterfly come turning through the air and settle on his arm. He picked it up. It was Gabriel's ticket to the Land of the Revolution.

Chapter 19

➤ Hector Bloom spent Sunday afternoon, Sunday night and most of Monday sleeping doubled up in the sperm-stained back seat of his convertible, waking only to grease his burns. He put off waking up. But sleep didn't work either: he dreamt he was swimming at night in a black ocean. He could see nothing. He could hardly breathe or move his arms and yet to stop would be to drown. He was sinking, his lungs filling with water, and a voice kept whispering, "The race, the race, the race!"

Hector woke in the shell of his automobile. It was day outside, late afternoon, with his friend dead and his love gone. He knew it would not be long before the cops came to search the woods where his car was parked. Wanting to go down kicking, he remembered that this was the day Robert Frank had named for his shutting-down of the main plant of Dewdrop Ltd. Hector went; it was the least he could do.

The plant stood out in the country on a double-track superhighway, nine miles from the University. At 5 P.M. Hector picked his way through file after file of cars waiting outside the plant just as they had waited by the gym two nights before. Finally he spotted a group of twenty or thirty people huddled by the gate. Save for Robert Frank and a few of Hector's fellow students, the group was mostly women and children. The children were young: blanketed and carried, pushed in carriages, clinging to their mothers' legs.

The people were lonely and few against the long expanse of wire fence. A silence hung over them; a faint, high-pitched metal whine seemed to penetrate their bones. A young man struck up on his guitar:

I'm gonna live the life
I sing about in my song.

I'm gonna stand for right
And all-ways shun the wrong.

I can't sing
One thing
And then do another.
It's day by day
and the Lord alone to cover.

I'm gonna live the life
I sing about in my song
Yes in my song.

Hector knew the young man and approached him, but there was no recognition. The young man's eyes were glazed and his fingers moved mechanically as he sang; he had been able to preserve himself only in a perpetual trance. His song was devoured by the silence as fast as it passed his lips.

Paul Felix was there, and his wife Christine knelt with their two children, trying to beat a tambourine. Paul Felix motioned with his eyes towards the guard box. At 5:30 the armed guards who watched them now so coldly would open the narrow gates and pass out a stream of 13,000 day-shift workers. The workers would come from the metal doors of the factory one-half mile back from the fence and flood across the open space and through the gate on their way to cars and supper.

The sun sank behind a cloud and the air grew colder. Clouds quickly massed and spread a roof of grey from horizon to horizon. In the windless cold the people crouched and pressed together on the gravel of the parking lot wet with melted snow. There was nothing to look at but iron fence and gravel and rows of cars, the low block buildings of the factory, and the concrete highway stretching out like the tracks of a brutal titan skier.

Closest to the gate stood Robert Frank, gazing implacably at the factory. Beside him were three cardboard boxes full of leaflets. Among other things, the leaflets informed the workers what they were working on. The new government project called for 10,000 nuclear missiles to be mounted on trailer trucks which would circle the highways of America so as to be invulnerable to Enemy retaliation. Each missile could destroy a city of people. Each truck would be commanded by a lieutenant—to give the order—and a sergeant—to throw the switch. Reading the leaflets, Hector imagined a certain truck parked for the night on the outskirts of a quiet Western town. Officer and man stumble home, having whiled the evening away at a public watering spot. He pictured them helping each other into the trailer. *Now where is that damn light switch?* CLICK CLICK.

Robert Frank looked up at Hector with his clear grey eyes. "Glad you could join us, Mr Bloom."

They shook hands. "What will you say to them?" Hector asked.

"What would you say?"

"I don't know. Face death: be beautiful."

"You sound like your poor friend."

Something must have changed in Hector's face.

"Yes," Frank said, "I heard about him. I was sad to hear it. A very great pity."

"No," said Hector.

"What's that?"

"No, not a pity."

Hector shrugged and stamped his foot in the gravel. Robert Frank turned his gaze back to the factory. He did not turn as three police cars and a small van pulled up behind them. The policemen kept their motors running and stayed watching in their cars. Perhaps Robert Frank would have turned to look if he had known that in the back seat of the first car sat Moses Mandel.

Moses spotted Hector Bloom and shook his head sadly. Hector was a nice boy; it was a shame he should be involved like this. He was tempted to send an officer to bring Hector to his car, but he had decided not to reveal himself unless a real incident occurred. The officers were well-trained—there was no reason to expect bad publicity.

Moses Mandel had other things to worry about. Without warning his Senator had informed him that his previously in-the-bag contract to manufacture Dewdrop domes for every large American city would probably be rejected. Congress had switched its enthusiasm to a sudden rival who proposed to set the cities in concrete blocks. All that had to be done was to provide air holes and passageways along the already-existing streets, and then the houses and buildings could be poured over with concrete just as they stood. The result would be a stupendous human beehive, impregnable to attack and rivaling the Enemy in efficiency of administration.

Probably even Dewdrop's original New York dome would be torn down—though already some newspapers were contending that the dome had never been there in the first place. As an old campaigner, Moses knew when he was licked; he had not even bothered to mobilize his employees in the Pentagon. But this missile contract had become—along with his new moonbird business—his bread and butter, and he couldn't afford to permit the slightest blemish on the Dewdrop missile image. He was there to protect Frank and his poor pacifists from harm. Moses sighed. They were like his children. You got no thanks from the very ones who needed you most.

Again he was surprised to see that big Hector Bloom. He had known of Hector's aversion for politics and thought of him as one who loved life and knew the score. Yet there Hector stood, side-by-side with Bobby Frank watching the distant doorway which would any minute open and slough forth Moses' employees.

The metal scream of the closing whistle gashed the air, as though the insides of the factory were scalded and crying out with steam. The children began to whimper. Heavy portals slid back and the workers poured forth, a broiling tangle of coveralled workers and tied-and-shirted engineers. As Robert Frank stepped forth with Hector, and the others followed, they heard behind their backs the unnerving cough of thousands of loyal autos revving up and snorting for the throttle. The workers marched untalking, holding portable radios blasting to their ears, their ranks broken here and there by foursomes of engineers playing bridge as they walked, adding schizoid chuckles and sniggers to the bilge wave of noise that froze the pacifists like quivering prairie dogs before an earthful of buffalo.

But Robert Frank was not afraid. He stepped forth bravely towards the oncoming masses, ready to let his feeling run like human blood and warm their hearts and brains.

As the front ranks came in range he smiled a proud democratic smile of friendship and good-fellowship, and the workers recoiled from the sheer ugly warmth of it. "I *will* love you!" Hector heard Frank murmur as he moved up to the very gates, leaflets in hand.

"Stop!" Frank called to the workers, and for an instant the seas parted, held fast by the force of Frank's love.

"Do you know what you are doing?" Frank asked them. "You're building certain death. You say you do it for your wives and children. But if you stop, your wives and children will not die. They will only die if you keep on."

Yes, thought Hector, *that's the game, how it is played and how it ends.*

"Better to stop," said Frank. "Nothing will happen."

Only the void will open, the void of freedom where there are no games. Or maybe we can't bear that. But yes better to stop and look at the void and make our games from that if we can.

Hector could sense that the mob was about to come alive, to move for Frank or against him. At the last second, Frank walked up to the nearest man and pushed towards him a brilliant white leaflet.

The man stood confounded; Hector saw his arm twitch, as if he were about to reach out to take the paper that was steadfastly offered him. But suddenly a frightened child screamed, and fell into sobs of inconsolable grief. Awakened, the man took the leaflet and smashed it down over Frank's head so that Frank stood there a clown in a collar of paper, and the men roared with sickly laughter and began to pass on by.

Chin held high, Frank pressed on into the oncoming tide of workers.

"Read this, friends," he called out in his clear voice. "It's a matter of life or death!"

The men stepped right around him. They wouldn't look into his eyes. Hector glanced behind him and saw policemen politely dragging away the women with their children. The mob was streaming by him now, gaining momentum as they headed for their cars and homes. Where at first they had stepped around him, now they brushed Hector rudely as if he weren't there. Hector was losing ground. "Take a leaflet!" he cried. "It won't hurt you, honest it won't. Take one just for fun!"

Still they came, pushing him back and away from Robert Frank.

I don't know how to play this game, Hector thought. *It will all be over before I learn.*

Gamely Hector lowered his shoulder and plunged on ahead, fighting his way towards Frank. Occasionally he blocked a worker and thrust a leaflet inside his coat collar.

Slipping and twisting along, Hector pulled up near Robert Frank. The older man was bobbing and weaving in the ocean of bodies; his head would disappear and then pop up again. Hector strained to see his face; Frank seemed to be wobbling strangely.

"Life and death, death and life!" Frank shouted. Hector was startled; the silver voice had cracked utterly. "Hurry up please," the old man shouted, "time ends soon." And then Hector heard a laugh that chilled his blood. He had never heard Frank laugh, never, and here it came again, shrill and terrible, knifing apart a lifetime of goodness.

"Tee hee hee hee hee," laughed Robert Frank. He lurched blindly this way and that as the workers shoved him out of their path. "Peace! Peace! Peace porridge hot!"

"I love you," he warbled, "love you to death! Peace porridge hot! Peace porridge cold!"

Frank was spinning dizzily, blowing kisses. Hector could not get to him. "I love you all!" the old man cried. Hector saw blood spurt from his ears. Then a shower of paper as the stricken agitator threw his burden to the heavens.

Hector was swept off his feet and carried thirty yards back by the thrust of the crowd. He crashed to the gravel head down, felt himself rolled and kicked along; writhing to right himself he was kicked in the head and blacked out. He came to on the gravel off to the side of the stream of march. Not far in front of him lay the body of Robert Frank. As he watched, the workers stepped over and around Frank, not even glancing down, some tumbling the body with their boots as they passed.

Hector jumped to his feet and charged up through the thinning crowd, swinging his elbows murderously. As he reached the body the last of the workers stepped over it and were gone.

"Hey you murderers!" Hector shouted. "Come back here and fight!"

The two guards left the gatehouse and waddled leisurely in his direction. One was chewing on a toothpick. A red screen came down before Hector's eyes; the blood in him leaped up in a charge of shame. He wanted to swing out for Gabriel, swing out for Olive, for Goose Jefferson, for mommy and daddy, for all souls lost and wasted. If the guards reached for their toylike pearl-handled guns he would seize them and crash their puffy heads together, stave in their florid faces, flay their jelly bodies and rend to shreds their uniforms.

The guards ambled closer, their cartridge belts untouched. They stared deadpan at the body. *One false move—*, thought Hector. Robert Frank lay with arms crossed and eyes wide open staring. A neat line of blood wrote silence in the snow of his leaflets.

One of the guards looked up at Hector. "Too much," he said, shaking his head. "Poor bastard. His heart must have busted."

The other guard started back toward the gatehouse. "I'd better call an ambulance," he said.

Hector turned away trembling. A red sun fell from the clouds and hung on the rim of the horizon. *You!* The voice from his dream shouted YOU YOU YOU YOU YOU.

His brain would burst itself. Before long: the game was just about over.

Hector reeled about, took the corpse of the pacifist up across his shoulders, and steadied himself alone against a setting sun. The weight and warmth of the body staggered him: what had this man done to have such awful substance in him? He had believed that men could be more than they are, that men could be men. *And died like a fool!*

Someone was tugging at his arm. He looked down and saw Moses Mandel, the dust on his face streaked with bulbous tears which welled from his eyes and trickled unevenly down the seams of his cheeks.

"Hector!" shrieked Moses. "This is ghastly! Ghastly!

That such a thing could happen! My god Bobby Frank that such a thing could happen! I didn't want this, Hector, I swear to you I didn't want this. It's one of those things, Hector!"

"Get away! Get away from me!" Hector pleaded.

"No, Hector, you've got to face it. Life is a horrid farce." Moses was croaking, hopping for Hector's attention in a grotesque chorus dance. "A horrid farce! A horrid farce! Life is a horrid farce! Death, Hector, Death! Death Death Death. It's ghastly, Hector, yes isn't it? Ha Ha: Everything in Life is Death!"

Hector booted the little man toward his waiting friends, and walked onward with his burden, moving slowly and separately away. He was going somewhere again. His hand clutched tight in his pocket around Gabriel's ticket to the Land of the Revolution. There it was: he would fly like a bird. He saw himself going golden as he climbed upward into the sun. He would turn and let the copper fire flash lightning in his feathers. And when the wax melted, and dribbled, as the blood was dribbling now, down between his shoulder blades, he would not fall to the sea and drown but spring free of his wings and climb and turn naked as a fish in the empty heavens. Perhaps our hero had become deranged, or had been so all along. That can happen these days when each man inside himself swears he is sane but from the outside who can tell? Only Hector Bloom, unlike many, was still alive, still on his feet and breathing, and he would get over it, *yes*. Or else he would never get over it. *Oh he would get over it.* He would get over it. Yes